Black-Eyed Peas and Cornbread

by

A. Jean Jackson

Dedication

To Mom (Aggie Jackson-Byers). Thank you for raising me to believe I could do anything, and that it was OK to do more than you had the opportunity to do.

This one's for you too.

Disclaimer

Though the area of Asheville called Eastend, and some of the streets refered to in this book truely exist, the characters in *Blackeyed Peas and Cornbread* are all ficticious. Any similarities to persons living or dead are coincidental.

Yvette
 you are such a special
lady. I am so glad to
know you. Enjoy this.
                    Jean 2017

PART 1

Located at the corner of Mountain and Pine Streets, Mae Mae's Eastend Cafe had a personality of its own. Placed literally at two forking roads, the cafe, like its owner seemed to demand attention, no matter which direction you approached.

Eastend sat at the backside of downtown Asheville, in the mountains of North Carolina. It was placed out of the way, so that Black folks could be seen and not heard. It was there to be conveniently nearby, but not in White folk's way. Above all else, Eastend was the center of many of the Black folk's world.

Two tall slendar doors greeted the customers at the cafe's entrance. The screened outer doors advertised Colonial Bread and RC Cola. The doors were the eyes of the cafe. They would take it all in, hold, warm, accept, no matter what, no matter who. They held inside the good and the bad of Eastend. They were the best friend who knew it all, but who could be trusted to remain silent.

Like a tall maple, Mae Mae towered way above the kitchen counter of the cafe. Her long graceful arms looked like limbs that could reach forever, as her slender hands touched and turned and kneaded biscuit dough with almost intimate familiarity.

The large, wooden rolling pin moved to the rhythm of the Gospel song that blasted on the jukebox. Mae Mae sang along in her alto voice as she

A. Jean Jackson

rolled out the dough and then cut out perfect circles one at a time. She usually insisted on making the fresh, hot, fluffy biscuits herself. No one else, not even Jimmie could make them to suit Mae Mae.

She sang louder as she placed each biscuit exactly one inch apart on the baking pan. Her eyes opened and closed, feeling the soul, the spirit of the song, yet seeing just enough to place the biscuits just right.

"Miss Mae," Jimmie said, entering the kitchen. "I thought you were leaving early tonight. I thought you wasn't feeling good."

She looked up, dodging that blast of heat from the oven as she placed the biscuits on the top rack. And in the midst of her singing, in the depths of her soulful praises to God, her profanity poured out just like Jimmie expected.

"And who in the Hell you think'll run this place if I go home," she said. "Yo' triflin' ass sure can't do it. Since when you worried about me goin' home anyway?"

She eased off, verbally retreating, leaving the chubby, baby faced Jimmie wondering what was wrong. He knew Mae Mae seemed to always dread going home. He knew that as long as the doors of the cafe were open, from sun up to the late night hours, she was always there. It was like the cafe was her whole life, her whole world. It was the one family member she had learned she could depend on.

"Miss Mae," Jimmie said, almost wishing for more of a fight. "I know this place ain't never the same

Black-Eyed Peas and Cornbread

without you. But it's gone be here. This place sure ain't going nowhere. I can handle things if you leave, you know that."

Mae Mae smiled showing beautiful dark, chiseled features seldom seen on a Black woman well into her forties. Her tall frame dwarfed Jimmie, as she stood quickly, just after checking the biscuits in the oven. She appreciated his concern, but they both knew she wasn't going anywhere.

As Jimmie gave in and left the kitchen Mae Mae followed his wide hips until he disappeared.
She hated his light coloring, and his big fat body. Every time she had to look at his face, it reminded her too much of Red. But his thoughtfulness, his genuine respect for her, made it hard for her to dislike him.

It was Sunday evening, and the dinner crowd was slowly drifting in. Lively, soulful, Gospel tunes still playing on the jukebox filled the dining room, changing the mood from the Saturday night jitterbug. On the Lord's day, Gospel was the only music you'd ever hear at Mae Mae's. But no matter what kind of music was playing, her profanity could always be heard way above the other low tones.

The lights were dim, as usual, but the light from the spinning beer ads hit the fading linoleum floor just enough to make it shine. Each faded black and white diamond shape on the floor formed a path leading into the heart of Mae Mae's and away from the realities in the outside world. A beer, good soul food, and Black folk's conversation, became their escape.

A. Jean Jackson

The kitchen door flapped open and Jimmie appeared. Music from the dining room intensified and poured in behind the open door. "What in the Hell are you doing, Jimmie?" Mae Mae asked, knowing Jimmie expected her to say something. "You know I doin't want you sittin' those dirty dishes there. Boy! You can't do shit right."

"Yes, Miss Mae," Jimmie said dutifully, but cursing under his breath. "I'll move them in a minute. I wanted to clear the sink first.

"By the way, this old man just came in. Says he wants to see you. His name is Looney, or something like that. I sat him in that booth in the back."

"Looney?" she said, needing to hold on to the counter for balance. "Oh my God! Looney is here?"

She walked slowly, part of her wanting to see him, part of her dreading the memories he'd bring. As if in slow motion, as if moving through a tunnel where no one else existed but her, she looked for him to appear out of the dimness of the room.

As she approached the booth, her eyes were fixed on the calendar hanging on the wall. Blond, beautiful Marilyn Monroe appeared on the calendar, watching each step as Mae Mae approached. The star's bright face, with pouting lips covered in red, and white hair like clouds, smiled as if it were meant especially for Mae Mae. It was like Marilyn understood.

The face in the darkness of the booth was old. It was much older than Mae Mae ever could have imagined. But the eyes were the same. The eyes took

Black-Eyed Peas and Cornbread

her back to a place she never wanted to go again.

Chapter 1

It was a hot steamy day in July 1919. Greenville, South Carolina was usually dry and dusty this time of year. But the constant steady rainfall that had smothered the earth for two long days was just too much for Cora Lee Gray to bear.

Water dripped steadily from the tin roof into the house, causing the misery of the outside to be much too real. The wetness inside and outside intensified the filth and the stench.

As usual, Cora Lee was in a bad mood. Putting up with seven children with one on the way was hell. So it made her feel better to curse. It was her God given right.

"What the hell you lookin' at?" Cora Lee shouted with pain illuminating her round, dark face.

"Nothin'," replied Mae Mae.

"Well, look like this damn baby comin'. Yo' daddy ain't here, so you goin' to have to help. Gone! Git them children out of here, and come on over here an help!"

"What you want me to do?" Mae Mae asked, really wanting to run away.

"Jus' help me, girl! Damn you! Damn the one that's comin' and damn the souls of all of you."

With each evil word that poured from Cora Lee's mouth, more of the baby's little head squeezed from her. Moments after the baby showed her little face to the world, she cried.

Cora Lee gladly freed herself, by tying and

cutting the cord. Everything was suddenly silent as Cora Lee looked down at her crying baby then searched out the dark, empty eyes of each of her seven other children. Seeing their blank indifference, she turned and faced the wall. It was her momentary escape from them all.

"Well Magg, look like you ain't the baby no more," said Suga the middle girl.

"Shut up girl," JoJo whispered. "Cora Lee gone get up from there an whip yo' butt."

"No she won't," soothed Mae Mae. "She need to rest some. We gone jus' sit here an be quiet for a while."

"Did you see it comin' out Mae Mae?" asked Sapp. "I ain't never looked til' this time. It sho' look nasty."

The children huddled together in the darkness of the small wood frame house. The fear in their eyes faded for the few moments Cora Lee stayed in bed. The warmth from their closeness made them feel safe. Just like the large, idle pot-bellied stove that sat in the middle of the floor, it nourished them and kept them alive. Even in the heat of summer, the dirty wood stove was like the true heart of the house.

At dusk, when the sun had almost disappeared, Mae Mae eased away from the dozing children and went to the porch. For her, standing on that rickety wooden porch with missing planks and rotten wood was like being on top of the world. From there she could see the perfect moon and wish on the stars.

A. Jean Jackson

There was a steady rhythm of the rain beating down on the tin roof. She closed her eyes and listened. The sound was calming. The tapping was like a special lullaby that she prayed her sisters and brothers could hear.

The smallness of the two-room shack held them all closer together. It bonded them from the time they were born, in a way they could never be with Cora Lee. Mae Mae was the oldest. She was the protector. Cora Lee was the enemy who marched around with her hands on her hips directing their lives. All of them hated her dark, round, smileless face.

Day by day and month by month the fall rains turned to the deep down coldness of winter. And with them praying for it all to end, the winter again turned slowly, relunctanly to spring. And with the spring always came changes. Even the mood of Cora Lee seemed to be changed.

"You take care of this baby so good," Cora Lee said with a big smile. "You must be wantin' one of yo' own."

"No Mama, I don't never want no babies. I jus' like takin' care of my brothers and sisters," said Mae Mae.

"Well anyway, I got me some plans for you. You ain't gone like it. But you'll get used to it. You'll be OK."

Mae Mae looked away, puzzled by Cora Lee's words. A few days later, Red arrived at the house to take her away.

Black-Eyed Peas and Cornbread

"Mae Mae, this here is Mr. Redman," said Cora Lee. "They calls him Red. Anyhow, you gone be goin' to live with him. You gone kind of be like his wife.

"He done paid right handsome for you, girl. See that big ole hog out yonder?" He gave me that hog in trade for you."

"Why Mama?" Why I got to go?" said Mae Mae, with tears welling in her eyes. "I don't know this man, Mama."

"Girl I done told you about questionin' me. Now you jus' do like I says. Jus' go. You gone be fine. Mr. Red gone take right good care of you."

Mae Mae looked at her long and hard, searching for some small sign of motherly love and compassion. She found none. Her mother's eyes were cold. The coldness pierced Mae Mae's heart, just like it always did. But this time was different. This time she knew her heart would never totally mend.

The dark distant eyes of her sisters and brothers watched her leave the only home she knew. No one spoke to her. They wondered in the silence of their minds if getting away from Cora Lee was what Mae Mae truly wanted. Deep down inside they knew Mae Mae's hell was just beginning.

The front porch where she had sat and dreamed while wishing on the stars, bid her goodbye. The only thing she left behind were tears. They fell to the ground and dried, in a place she would never see again.

In the months that followed Mae Mae quicky discovered that living with Red was a fate worse than death. From the beginning she realized that Red was worse than Cora Lee could ever be. With Red she quickly realized that her body, her innocense was at stake. Nothing, not even her body belonged to her.

Nightfall captured the last light of evening, bringing with it the certainty that soon Red would be home. As Mae Mae scrubbed the floor absentmindedly, she gazed at the greyness of the water trickling to a single drop. Scrubbing the floor reminded her of him. Neither he nor the floor would ever be clean enough for her.

She hated the old run down sharecropper shack that she was forced to live in. It was larger than Cora Lee's. But something was missing here. A dark, cold loneliness drifted over this house like a cloud. It was intensified by the absence of her brothers and sisters.

The constant coldness in the air drifted deep down into her bones. Whatever season it was, no matter how much heat the big stove was putting out, or how much the sun fought to come through, it never got warm enough.

But what she hated most was the smell. Red's poignant smell stayed with her always. It was like the invisible chains that held her captive.

The huge wooden door squeaked loudly as Red staggered into the room He lifted the lid of the stove and spit at the flames. Mae Mae could feel his eyes burning into the back of her. She continued scrubbing, waiting.

Black-Eyed Peas and Cornbread

"Didn't I tell yo' ass I want yo naked and in that bed waitin' for me this time of night?" Red shouted, as he pulled back to strike and knocked her to the floor.

"Ah! Yessir Mr. Red," Mae Mae replied, trying to block her head. "I was jus' tryin' to finish this so it'll be clean in the mornin'."

A warm stream of blood rolled down through her hair, and stopped at the base of her neck. She didn't realize it was there until the redness appeared on the hand that searched out the pain.

"You jus' stop all that pretendin' like you hurtin'. I'll give yo' ass somethin' to holler about. Gone! Git in that bed anyway. I'm gone fuck you tonight, jus' like I do any other night. I don't care nothin' about you hurtin'."

Pulling herself up slowly from the floor, Mae Mae started a slow, careful walk towards the bed. Before she could get there, Red hit her again. Diving to reach the bed, she laid on her side and doubled over with her knees tight to her chest. Red approached the bed and slapped her across the face.

Her tongue reached for the blood in the corner of her mouth, as Red mounted her body. The taste of her own blood was a relief. The saltiness, the warmth of it calmed her.

Pain became her friend and her enemy as she prayed for the point where numbness always took over her body. The numbness was like being in limbo. It was like an escape from all of the evil in her life. It helped her to become the whore that she needed to be to make life bearable.

A. Jean Jackson

"Mr. Red," she whispered into the dark cold air, as she pushed her breasts close to his body. "Can I touch you? Before he could answer, she had his throbbing penis in her hand. He was breathing hard, as she massaged him softly, yet powerfully.

Red moaned loudly as Mae Mae took control of every inch of his body. In the heat of passion he turned to kiss her. But she denied him the softness of her smooth, dark lips. Fear was always her companion; but not here, not now, not in bed.

As he lingered on the fringes of sexual insanity, she finally let him enter her. The warmth of his hard penis penetrated her as she tried to dismiss any pleasure she might feel. He grabbed her hips, clawing, pushing his dirty nails into her sides.

Their sex became a battle of wills. He wanted to climb inside of her to capture her soul. She wanted to control, letting him have nothing but what she chose to give. It was the one battle she always won.

The mixture of smells, the wetness, the moans, the unwanted touches played constantly in Mae Mae's head. The heavy weight, the shaking, the shifting seemed impossible for her to take another time. But she did. She always had to.

She felt the burden of his rolls of fat shifting upon her as he ground deeper and deeper into her. His sweat this night, as with every night, poured onto her small round breasts. She hated his liquids. She hated how they seemed to surround her, entrap her. They were everywhere he moved. She could not escape them.

Black-Eyed Peas and Cornbread

The dark coffee color of her smooth skin glistened in the moon light, as she glanced up at his closed eyes. "A devil like him ought to never close they eyes," she thought to herself. "Somebody libel to kill his ass."

Moaning loudly, he reached his peak without her. She refused to go there with him. She refused to ever enjoy what they did together.

The heavy calm rhythm of his breathing after sex, signaled safety for her. It was her time to be by herself, to nurse her wounds, to calm her fears, to think, to pray, to cry.

Slowly, quietly she eased out of bed and went to the window. At this time each night the window became her key to the rest of the world. Whenever she opened it, it formed her own private path to the moon.

The moon seemed to smile down at her like a needed friend. It was as if in it's eminent wisdom, the moon was telling her to be patient. It was like it knew something she didn't.

The cold air coming through the closed window sent a chill down her body as she hugged her shoulders. She looked over at Red, reluctant to return to his unpleasant yet warm body. She glanced back out of the window, enjoying a final moment of distance from the bed and from him.

As always, morning came much too quickly. When her sleep finally took her far away from him, the morning always forced her immediate return. Reluctantly she rose and went to the outhouse.

A. Jean Jackson

The dirty blue robe she threw on drug the ground as she stumbled down the two rickety stairs of the front porch. She pulled the robe tighter to shield herself from the cold. The frost from her breath circled in the air in front of her. It mingled slowly with the outhouse odor that greeted her each morning.

The sound of her dripping pee echoed below her as she waited for the last drop to fall its distance into the hold in the ground. Her tall thin frame stood, just missing the roof. A beautifully carved, perfect nose on dark smooth, almost flawless skin, turned up in disgust as she walked away to the sound of the slamming wooden door.

She eased quietly into the house. Red stared but said nothing. Hungry flames from the stove jumped towards her as she tossed in the last piece of wood and quickly closed the lid. As she wiped her hands on her robe, she moved to the other side of the room. "When you gone git my breakfast girl?" shouted Red with a blow to the side of Mae Mae's head.

"I'm gone git you something', Mr. Red," she said, not even blinking from the pain.

"You fixin' hoe cakes with that?"

Yessir."

"Well hurry yo' ass up an git it over here. You be this late with it next time, I'm gone beat yo' ass. You hear me?"

Finally, just quick enough to avoid a slap to the face, she placed his food on the crooked, thick legged wooden table. Hot liver mush, eggs scrambled in butter, grits, and baked hoe cakes quickly disappeared from his plate. Crumbs fell from his mouth, as he chewed.

"It tast jus' like shit," he said, leaning back sucking his teeth, belching.

She looked down at the floor with big sad eyes. Long dark hair, braided and pinned at the top of her head, sat like the crown of a young innocent princess. But as she stared at him push from the table, she cursed him.

The door slammed as Red departed with an absent grunt. Mae Mae waited for a moment, then ran to the window to watch the distance grow between them. As he disappeared from view, she breathed a sigh of relief.

She ran outside to the porch in search of fresh air. The beautiful bright blue sky forced a smile to her face as she looked about savoring the few moments of freedom.

Leaning on the banister of the porch, enjoying the absence of her captor, Mae Mae heard a sound."What was that?" she whispered under her breath, in search of the strange sound. Silence fell. Then she heard it again.

As she moved closer to the sound, she spotted a cat surrounded by five kittens laying under the porch. They laid contently in the dirt space under the steps.

"Hey little ones," Mae Mae said with a smile. "I sure didn't know what was makin' that noise under there. How in the world ya'll end up under these ole rickety steps?

A. Jean Jackson

"You better git back over there with everybody else," Mae Mae said softly to one of the kittens. "Yo' mama gone make sure you git some milk."

She rubbed the wandering kitten's head as she brought him close to her chest. "You the runt ain't you? But you still my favorite."

The next day, the runt was the only one left. The she cat and the rest of the litter were no where to be found.

Located a few yards from the house, the big door of the wooden shed creaked as Mae Mae opened it and went inside. The cold hardness of the dirt floor brought on a chill as she moved with the kitten to the middle of the room.

"Yo' mama didn't want you either," she said, with tears in her eyes. "But that's alright. You and me gone be jus' fine. We gone take care of one another. I'm gone call you Blackie, OK?"

Tears fell silently on the dirt floor as she wiped them with the back of her hand. As Blackie drifted off to sleep in her lap, she quietly she placed him on a pile of rags and tipped away.

Pretty soon, the heat of summer dominated the days while the evening air was a constant reminder of the cool, calm beauty of spring. Though the sun seldom penetrated the dense woods surrounding the house, Mae Mae welcomed the little bit of warmth that arrived in spite of it.

It was a warmth that revived her soul. It prepared her for the dark coldness that snuck in with the fall and overwhelmed her in the dreadful winter months.

The sunset arrived in the evening an showed its magnificent colors. Mae Mae listened to the calm steady purring of Blackie and breathed in the perfection of the moment.

They sat mesmerized by the bright orange color of the sun settling in the trees. It peeped through the few spaces in the woods, determined to be seen before it retired. With it came the slight chill of the evening air.

"That's sure enough a pretty sunset, Blackie," Mae Mae said. "Don't thank I ever seen one like that before."

They sat in silence with her answer floating in the air, as darkness crept up and captured the night. "Guess I'm gone go in now," Mae Mae said, standing to enter the house. "Go on now, Blackie. See you in the mornin'."

The kitten waddled away reluctantly, turning back to look at her. "Night Blackie," she whispered across the yard. "You my best friend."

The next morning Mae Mae awoke to the sound of an owl outside of the window. The chill in the morning air attacked her as she climbed out of bed. She noticed Red was already up as her feet hit the cool wooden floor.

"What you got out there in that shed, girl?" Red said, smiling the smile that highlighted his brown light colored eyes.

"What you meanin' Mr. Red," Mae Mae said. "I

ain't got nothin' out there."

"I seen that damn cat."

Mae Mae was silent. She ran frantically across the yard to the shed. The door squeaked open as she peeked inside. She walked to Blackie's pile of cloth.

Her heart stopped at the moment she found him. His blank eyes stared at her from the darkest corner of the shed. He fell limp in her arms as she picked him up. Blood dripped to the ground landing silently on the dirt floor. His head fell to one side showing the fatal slash to his throat.

Mae Mae's loud scream echoed off the walls of the small shed as she ran out into the morning air. She ran out and upward through the darkened woods.

She climbed until she was exhausted. There was no place to go but up. She climbed up out of the depths of hell.

Chapter 2

"This place must be heaven," Mae Mae said as she looked around at the perfect shades of blue and white floating in the sky. "It's the prettiest place on this earth."

Wild flowers were everywhere around her painting the landscape with their delicate beauty. Their bright purple and yellow colors smiled and welcomed her.

The sun was touching her face warming her, like it never had before. Its rays surrounded her like this was the only place on earth it ever touched. It made her happy.

Blackie laid beside her with a certain aura of peace surrounding him. Old tears rolled quietly down her cheeks and dried in the ray of sunlight that was touching her face.

Blackie's soft black fur felt like he was still alive. But there was a cold stiffness that had taken over his body. There was nothing she could do to make him move. His eyes stared blankly back at her. Their usual hint of animation was gone. Nothing was there. Blackie was dead and she could do nothing to help him.

A peacefulness that seemed to arrive with the rays of sunlight crept into Mae Mae's heart. She heard a voice inside of her head say, "And what better place than here?" Looking all about her she smiled. With an energy that came from nowhere, she dug a shallow grave. She placed Blackie in his rags, put him

A. Jean Jackson

into the ground and walked away.

When she returned home, the house was quiet until the door slammed with the arrival of Red. His smell filled the room as Mae Mae began to sing. *"I come to the garden alone, while the dew is still on the roses. An the voice I hear, fallin' on my ear..."*

"What's yo, ass sangin', gal?" Red shouted. "Don't be sangin' that church stuff in my house, you hear!"

"Yessir," she said, still humming in her head.

Later that night as she laid in bed wishing for his orgasm to arrive and release her, she prayed. "I'm gone try to forgive him Lord. 'Cause I know that's what you teaches. I need a lot of help with tryin' not to hate Red, Lord. Can't nobody help me with that but you.

"An the joy we share as we tarry there. None other have ever knowed," she hummed again, looking away as he finally climaxed.

A squirrel scampered up a tree followed closely in chase by another one. Birds scattered in every direction causing Mae Mae to look about in wonderment at the sudden excitement. Amused, she smiled then calmed the birds with her singing.

"That was nice. Sang some more," a smiling voice shouted from behind the trees.

Mae Mae turned around searching for the voice. "Who that?" she shouted.

"Don't mean to scare you or nothin'," the man said as he stepped forward. "I been seein' you come here for a long time. Jus' thought it's about time I said somethin'. Seem like yo be likin' this place much as I do."

"Yeah, Yeah," Mae Mae said stuttering. "I, I love it here. Sure didn't know nobody else knew nothin' about it though."

The man laughed throwing his head way back, as his beautiful white teeth contrasted his sun soaked complexion and the flowing black hair draped about his wide shoulders. High, proud cheekbones carved perfectly into his strong face, invited her eyes to look closer.

"Well I ain't gone fight about whose place this was first," he said still smiling. "Guess we gone have to jus' share it. By the way, my name Jacob. But they call me the Injun'."

"Mae Mae my name," she said shyly, looking down. "I live down the hill a piece with Mr. Red."

"Yeah. Yeah I know," said Jacob, looking away. "I seen where you go when you leave here."

"This place is 'paradise' to me," she said, with a firm determined voice. "It's the place I come to git away from hell. I come here for peace and quiet."

"OK! OK!" Jacob said with a hearty laugh. "I ain't gone stand in the way of yo' peace an quiet. You come here jus' like you been doin'. I ain't gone bother you."

Jacob's words still hung in the air, as Mae Mae left him standing and walked away. She disappeared into the trees as his eyes followed. It was months before she saw him again.

A. Jean Jackson

"Boo!" he shouted, smiling the smile that had haunted her since the first time she saw him.

Mae Mae jumped awake. Looking up seeing the glistening white teeth surrounded by a halo of sunlight, she smiled. "Why you tryin' to scare me to death," she said.

"Jus' playin' with you.," said Jacob. "I was watchin' you the whole time you was comin' up the hill. In fact, I been seein' you a whole lot more than you think. See, tol' you I wasn't gone mess up yo' peace an quiet."

"Yeah, you did say that."

"Besides I jus' like lookin' at you. Don't have to be sayin' nothin'. You the most beautiful woman I ever seen."

"Thank you," she said, looking down, embarrassed. "Is you full injun?" she asked, squinting, blocking the sun with her hand.

"No," he said softly. "I'm mostly injun', but I got some of everything in me. My mama, she's injun mixed with colored. Might have had some white in her too. Hell, to me it don't make no diff'rence. My daddy, he was pure dee Cherokee. Guess I took most of my looks after him.

"What about you? You mixed or what?" he said, looking at her coffee brown skin and the long dark hair pinned to the top of her head.

"I don't know Jacob," she said, with sadness capturing her face. "I don't know much about my family. My mama sol' me away. That's how I ended up here with Mr. Red. He paid for me with a ole dirty

Black-Eyed Peas and Cornbread

hog."

"Oh no, Mae Mae!" Jacob said, almost dumbfounded. How could a mother do that? He looked for a long time into her sad face. Their eyes came together touching, comforting without words. Mae Mae turned away, frightened by the closeness.

"I hope we can be friends," Jacob said, touching her hand. "I think you need one."

"Yeah," she said, with tears in her eyes. "I ain't had one in a long, long time.

Following those words, she gently pulled away from his hand and she went down the hill. An indescibable happiness went with her. Each time she saw Jacob it became harder and easier to go home to Red.

They met in 'paradise', and came together briefly from their totally different lives. Neither of them knew what drew them there. Whatever it was, neither of them could stop it. Jacob became her friend, her confidante, her world.

"What's wrong Mae Mae?" Jacob asked, when she jumped to his touch. "Did I hurt you?"

"No, no it wasn't you, Jacob.

"Did he hurt you Mae Mae? Did Red hurt you?"

"Yeah."

"My God! Mae Mae," he said, as he gently took her in his arms. I could kill him. An I will if he hurts you like this again."

"No Jacob! Don't talk like that. Promise me, Jacob.

"I can't stand to see you like this. But I'll do

what you say Mae Mae. I love you."

"I love you too Jacob," she said softly, not knowing where the words were coming from.

Their lips met in an uncontrollable fit of passion. He could feel every inch of her soft dark lips, as he lingered there enjoying the wet thickness. He lightly caressed her back wanting to heal the wounds with his touch.

They made love for the first time, surrounded by the natural beauty of their own 'paradise'. His tall muscular body brought total pleasure to her, as he touched every part of her body.

Mae Mae screamed in ecstasy anxious for him to enter her. She took him into her, unable to live another moment without him. They climaxed together with voices that rang out and echoed in the trees.

"Don't move," Jacob said in a soft soothing voice. "I want to stay here fo'ever an die in yo' arms."

"Jacob! Don't say that. Don't never say that."

"Sorry," he said. "It jus' ain't never been like that before. Never."

"I know."

"Why you stay with him, Mae Mae? If all he do is hurt you all the time, why don't you jus' leave?"

"I don't know Jacob," she said softly, pausing at the top of the hill. "One of these days I'm gone find my way. I'm gone be a real person one day."

They kissed, holding on to the moment, not wanting to let go. Finally, Mae Mae broke away, knowing what awaited her down the hill. As they parted, a special longing that neither of them had ever felt before went with them.

Her only reason for living, for existing was to be with Jacob. When she could not be with him, her mind was constantly on him. She was consumed by him.

The shadows on the walls bounced about her playfully, animated by the lively flames in the kerosene lamp. Mae Mae smiled, amused by the patterns in front of her. She welcomed the slight darkness in the room. In the darkness, her eyes were free to show the love she held secret in her heart.

Red ventured over looking down on her, sucking his teeth. He stared at her for what seemed an eternity. Mae Mae breathed irregularly as she looked down at his feet, nervously awaiting whatever the moment would bring.

"I hear Cora Lee dead," he said, matter-of-factly. "Guess yo' black ass don't give a shit though. You ain't never cared nothin' about yo' mama."

Emotions filled her heart and flooded her eyes, as she refused to blink the wetness away. Whatever it was she felt for Cora Lee, Red would never know. She said nothing. She climbed into bed and performed just as expected.

The next day she headed for 'paradise' more anxious than ever to see Jacob. Her heart hurt from the news of Cora Lee more than she ever believed it could. She needed to talk. She needed to lighten the weight that was tugging at her soul.

"Red sayin' my mama, Cora Lee done died,"

A. Jean Jackson

Mae Mae said to Jacob when he finally arrived.

"How you feel about that Mae Mae?" he said. "You ain't talked about yo' mama much. Only thing I know, you say she sol' you to Red.

"You love yo' mama, Mae Mae? How ever you feel, you can tell me."

Her mind faded behind the wetness forming in her eyes. The tears flooded forth as if trying to wash away her pain.

"No Jacob. I guess I ain't never loved Cora Lee. Jus' like she ain't never loved me."

Jacob held her close with the strength in his muscular arms squeezing, trying to take away the pain. But when he searched out her eyes, all of the hurt and sorrow of her short life was still there. Not even the pure depths of his love could take it away.

"I don't like bein' sad when I'm here with you Jacob. Let's talk about something happy. Tell me about yo' mama. What was she like Jacob?"

His arms pulled her closer to him as she sat on the ground between his legs near the big rock. With a big smile and eyes that twinkled with delight, he looked towards the sky and recalled his mother.

"Her name Auwee. I don't know what that mean though. It's a injun name, I know that much. She a beautiful woman, jus' like you.

"Her hair is as white as a fresh snow in the twilight of evenin'. It flow straight down her back. She got dark copper skin like me. Her eyes so deep brown you can see down into her snow-white soul.

"You ever seen anybody that got wise hands,

Mae Mae?" he said, still looking towards the sky as he spoke.

"No, No Jacob, I ain't," said Mae Mae listening intently.

"Well, Auwee's hands is wise. It's something about them that shows wisdom. They long an slender an they move light and smooth. She seem fragile on the outside, but them hands got strength an power that come from out of no where.

"Her features in the face a lot like yours. They sharp an carved like most injuns'. She kind of short. But she still a leader among her people.

"I growed up in the mountains near the apple orchards. I was the only boy. But I had three sisters too. All of them live right around there in a village near the orchards. They ain't never ventured far from there.

"We growed up po' jus' like all the folks around there. But Mama Auwee was so full of love we ain't never felt we was missin' nothin'. I ain't never knowed nothin' but love."

"Jacob, my heart happy for you," Mae Mae said.

"Now, my heart belong to you," he said, pointing to his muscular chest. "You ain't never got to worry about bein' loved again."

They held on to each other as if for pure survival. Their hearts beat in a perfect unison, while they kissed, fearing the moment when they would be forced to part again.

They left, but they always returned. An by the end of summer, the path they trod towards 'paradise' was well worn. For Mae Mae, the path only went in one direction.

Fall arrived showing its colors. The flowers of spring and of summer had long since faded making way for the magnificent show of the colorful leaves.

After several days of heavy rain the sun finally arrived. It peeped in and out from behind the clouds, teasing her. Then it decided to stay for a while, smiling down like an old man coming back from a needed rest.

Days without seeing Jacob left her yearning for him in a way she had never felt before. She was overwhelmed by her need to see him as she started up the hill. Seldom touched by the drying warmth of the sun, the path was muddy as she climbed. By the time she reached the top she was out of breath.

"Jacob ain't here yet?" she said to herself. "Most times he be here before me."

There was a rustling in the woods. Mae Mae jumped as she looked towards the sound. In the fog it was hard to see. But after a moment she relaxed, relieved by the sudden appearance of a squirrel.

Then, like out of a wonderful dream, she looked up at the sky and Jacob was there. His broad shoulders stood over her like a huge oak. Eyes that penetrated her soul glared down at her. She pulled him to meet her.

"Lord! How I missed you," she said, as they kissed.

Jacob said nothing. He caressed her body slowly, sensually with his large gentle hands. Both of them moaned with delight. Each wanting to capture the other's soul. Each wanting to give it away.

With eyes closed they savored their pleasure, not wanting the moment to end. They reached their sexual peak together, no longer able to control their passion.

There was complete silence. The whole of 'paradise' was completely still. Then, before either of them realized that they were not alone, Jacob suddenly felt cold steel pressing against the side of his head.

"Boy! You ever thank you was gone die right after fuckin' like that?" Red asked, with a smile on his face, and a rifle in his hand.

"Go back to the house, girl," Red shouted, still holding the gun on Jacob.

Mae Mae rose then turned to Jacob and held on pressing her head to his bare chest. Red jerked her away slinging her to the ground with his free hand. When she rose again he slapped her, drawing blood.

The taste of her blood erased all of her fear as she ran towards Red and stood between the gun and the two men. Slowly, she raised her hands to the sky and shouted, "Take me Lord! Take Me! Please! Please! Mr. Red," she said, hysterically. "I'll do anything. Jus' don't kill him. Please!"

With tears in his eyes and utter defeat in his face, Jacob pleaded with her to leave. He pleaded as if he knew it was his final request. "Go on Mae Mae!" he said softly. "Always remember how much I love you."

"You better git on down the hill girl and hope I don't kill yo' black ass," Red shouted to Mae Mae.

Reluctantly she turned and started towards the path and down the hill. She refused to look back. "I'm gone love you forever, my Jacob," she shouted up to the trees.

Deep in the darkness of the forest, she stopped and closed her eyes as a blast from the gun echoed in her ears...

Chapter 3

There was complete silence. Nothing and no one could be seen on the road for miles. The sporadic sound of crickets in the distance was the only assurance that she was not in the world alone. A huge hawk soaring overhead caught her attention. "Jus' like that bird," Mae Mae said aloud. "I'm gone be free."

After a long while, the sound of a loud sputtering motor broke through the silence. When Mae Mae caught sight of the old broken down pile of junk, and the man who was driving it, her heart pounded with excitement.

A small, dark, bearded man, with rotten front teeth, stopped the truck and peered from the window. He grinned widely and then spat a stream of tobacco.

"Where 'bouts you goin', Missy," the dark, smiling man called out to Mae Mae. "I'm goin' up da mountain a piece to Asheville," he said, not waiting for an answer. "Thank dat'll hep ya some?"

"Yessir," Mae Mae replied.

"Get on in den. Name's Looney. What yorn?"

"Mae Mae. My name Mae Mae," she said shyly.

"So, what a young gal like you doin' out here all by yo'self?" Looney asked, behind another stream of tobacco juice. "I ain't meanin' to meddle or nothin'" he added. "But it look like you been hurt. Why yo' face all swol'?"

She looked away, ashamed of the bruises.

A. Jean Jackson

"No, no I ain' t hurt that bad," she said, looking down at the floor. "But I'm runnin' away from the man I was married off to."

"You married?" Looney asked, scratching his head, holding his dirty hat in the same hand. "You don't look no more 'n a chile."

"I'm just turnin' eighteen," she said. "I been wit that man over four years. We ain't never went before no preacha' or nothin'. But my mama give me to him when I was near about thirteen. She traded me away for a hog."

"A damn hog! Yo' mama gave you to some man, fa a hog?"

"Yeah, she gave me to a man name of Red. He mean as hell an he beat me every single day of my life. I had to get away before he killed me."

"Sound like you done had a hard life lil' gal." Looney said, after a long silence. "Men who beats up on women, ain't fit fa livin' on dis' earth. I gits drunk sometime, but I ain't never raised my han' to no woman."

After a short silence, carefully selecting his words, Looney spoke again. "My mama was black as coal, and big as a horse. Mos' folks ain't thought she's pretty o' nothin'. But daddy loved ha. He loved da groun' she walked on.

"My daddy used to say dat men's got to respec' dey women. Colored women done had hard times. Dey menfolk ain't 'spose to be tearin' 'em down."

Looney talked on and on as he drove with Mae Mae seated beside him. But his words drifted past her, as her mind lingered on Red. Thoughts of the hell she'd just escaped haunted her. The picture of Red's gun pressed to her head kept playing over and over in her brain.

She remembered the door squeaking. Red entered holding a gun still warm from the shots fired moments before. Approaching her with a blank look on his face, he pointed it at her head and without hesitating, he pulled the trigger.

Mae Mae prayed to die. But the blast that she hoped for faded to a mere click. Her eyes remained closed, but she could feel his body close to her. She could feel the warmth of his breath. She felt his fists as they made contact with her face. But she did not feel a thing.

The pain and the fear that was present in the room seemed to awaken Red's desires. Her heartbeat, her breathing was under his control. Before she knew it, he forced her to the floor. He tore off the thin cotton dress that covered her body. She closed her eyes wishing she were dead as he raped her.

Swollen, bruised eyes glared at him as he reached his peak. Afterwards, he rolled over and fell into a deep sleep. It was the sleep that would set her free.

"Free," she said aloud, as the calmness of Looney's voice recaptured her attention. "Red ain't gone never hurt me no more."

"I'm gone try ta help you gal," Looney said, as the old truck trudged up the steep mountain. "I know dis woman, name o' Mizz Letty, in Asheville. She own

A. Jean Jackson

a boardin' house. When we git dere, I'm gone take you ta her. She'll try ta do what she can fa you. She a straight up Christian woman."

Mae Mae's eyes glared at him with disbelief. It was hard to imagine that this toothless, old, dirty man, driving a truck full of tobacco would be the one to help her to freedom.

"Why you wantin' to help me?" she said, forcing the words from her mouth. "You don't know me. You ain't never seen me before in yo' life."

Looney said nothing. He just looked at her as the golden glow of the morning sun, rising over the mountains, danced on his face. Without words, he calmed her heart. A feeling of peace drifted through her entire body, letting her know that everything was going to be alright.

As she sat beside him, amidst all of the stench around them, she had no doubt. He had been sent to rescue her from hell.

The mountains were beautiful, as the old truck pulled and jerked and strained upward. As they climbed, the unbelievably blue sky greeted Mae Mae with the smile of a new mother. The emerald green trees and the distant rolling hills were like hands folded in prayer.

Mae Mae twisted and turned taking it all in. she closed her eyes, and for the first time since she ran away, she truly felt her freedom...

"Hey lil' gal! Lil' gal, you a'right," the old man shouted, with Mae Mae still staring down at him in the cafe's back booth. "You know who I am, don't you?"

"Looney! My God, Looney!" she said, joyfully hugging him with her long slender arms. "I knowed it was you. I jus' knowed it. Lord, I ain't seen you in about a hundred years.

"I know Missy," he said, followed by his wonderful toothless laugh. "It have been a while, ain't it.

"I remembers the firs' time I seed you. You wont nothin' but a chile. You was talkin' 'bout you was runnin' 'way from yo' husban'. What his name? Oh Yeah! Yeah! Name o' Red, wont he?"

"Yeah," Mae Mae said with sadness in her voice. "Looney, so much done happened since that day you dropped me on Mizz Letty's door step. Lord that was over forty years ago. I wont but 'bout eighteen years old back then.

"Lord Looney, where in the world my manners? I know you must be tired and hungry. How about lettin' me treat you to a bite to eat?"

She took him by the hands and looked deeply into his eyes as the gentle light over the booth formed a halo over his head. The shallow lighting over the booth was there to guard the secrets they had between them.

They remained silent for a long time, as they privately recaptured the emotions of the past. She stared at the changes that age had forced on him. And Looney watched as her long slender fingers traced the initials E.R. loves F.J., carved deeply into the top of the wooden table.

A. Jean Jackson

"Looney, you didn't know I had a boy and a girl did you?" she asked, breaking the silence. I ain't sat here in so long I forgot Esther's initials was here. Lord! I miss that girl, Looney. I miss her real bad."

"Where she at Missy? Why she ain't here wit' you?"

Before she could answer, they were startled by Jimmie's sudden entrance from the kitchen. The urgent movement of Jimmie's feet clicked quickly across the worn black and white linoleum floor.

"Mizz Mae, Elijah in the back talkin' 'bout he need to see you," Jimmie said, looking curiously at Looney. "He scared to come in here. You know you told him not to be comin' in here askin' for nothin' no more."

"O.K Jimmie," she said. "I'll go an see what he want. He probably jus' wantin' some money.

"Looney meet Jimmie. Jimmie my cook," she said as she turned to leave. "Jimmie, brang my ole friend Looney a big plate of chittlin's an a big ole piece of that hot cornbread. You need anything else Looney, jus' let Jimmie know. I'll be right back."

She walked away slowly, knowing what awaited her. The bright red torn and tattered bar stools in a perfect line across the bar directed her to the kitchen.

As she walked into the room, Elijah stood staring with eyes so like his father that she turned away.

"Hey Ma," he said, looking down. "How you been doin'?"

Black-Eyed Peas and Cornbread

"Yo' ass don't care nothin' about how I been doin'," she said. "What you want, Elijah?"

"I know you tol' me not to be askin' no more, Ma. But I need to borrow some money. Not much! An I swear I'm gone pay you back this time. I swear."

"What kind of trouble you in this time boy. You ain't been nothin' but trouble to me since the day you was born. I'm gone stop payin' yo' keep. I wish you'd jus' let me be."

"Come on Ma. If it was Esther, you'd give her whatever she want. Jus' like you always did."

"I done told you boy! Don't go throwin' Esther up in my face. Compared to you, that girl a angel. An I still believe you done something to make her leave."

"I didn't do nothin' to that girl. She jus' left. She left 'cause she was tired of yo' shit. That's why. Now! You gone give me the money or not?"

She reached for the handkerchief pinned to the inside of her dress between her breasts. Unrolling it, she pulled out several bills and handed them to him. "Here," she said. "Now get out o' my face."

With a smile of victory, Elijah left through he back door and disappeared into the darkness of Eastend. Mae Mae stood quietly and listened until the sounds of his footsteps faded away.

As she returned to Looney, her troubling thoughts showed in her eyes. But within a few seconds they disappeared behind her smile.

"How those chittlins, Looney?" she said. "Can I bring you somethin' else?"

"No, No gal. I'm gittin' full as a tick. You cook

A. Jean Jackson

these thangs, Missy? Seem like you learned some o' that good ole mountain cookin' from Letty. That was one cookin' lady!"

"Yeah. Yeah Looney, you right about that. I learned everything I know from Ma Letty. When you dropped me off on her doorstep, that was the best thing anybody ever done for me."

She watched the movement of his toothless gums enjoying the soft meaty flavor of her chitterlings. As she watched him, her thoughts turned to Ma Letty...

It was the kind of day that Ma Letty would have loved. She loved the spring. The newness, the constant surprises, the breathtaking beauty always brought a special glow to her face. But at the end of spring in 1940, the glow of her face would never be seen again. It was the day of her burial.

A powerful voice poured forward from behind the podium. His short, small frame made him barely visible. But he held the attention of his entire congregation.

"Letty Brown," Reverend Hennessy said, almost shouting. "Letty Brown was placed on this earth, in this town, in the Eastend community for a reason.

"You see! My Father has a plan for us all. An his plan my brothers an sisters, was to place this fine woman right here with us.

"An ain't we glad," he said, dancing around the podium. "I said! Ain't we glad!"

Black-Eyed Peas and Cornbread

"Amen! Amen!" shouted the ushers standing in the aisles.

"Yes!" he began, after a dramatic pause. "We was truly blessed by her presence in our lives. I can't think of another human being who so clearly fit here and belonged here like she did. Yes! He had a plan, and thank God we was here to be so blessed by that plan.

"Seem like to me, ain't nobody sitting here in this church blood related to Mizz Letty. But guess what!" he said with a skip. "All of us is her family."

"Preach! Preach!" called out Deacon Johnson, with both arms waving in the air.

"I guess what I'm trying to say today," he said, in a calm low voice. "I'm telling you that in some way Letty Brown touched us all.

"You know," he said, with a chuckle. "There's some lost folks sometimes in this world. An I think people just like Letty Brown was put here on earth for them. She was put here to love 'em. To show them the way. To be the family they never had.

"That's why she owned that boarding house. That's why strangers, and lost souls could go to her and find love and support. She became the guardian angel to them all.

"And I know today she would not want us to dwell on how she died, but on how she lived. Don't think about that dreadful fire that burned her up as she lay helpless in her bed. Don't think about her house burning down to the ground while her loved ones were forced to watch. She wouldn't want that.

A. Jean Jackson

"Think of the love she gave us all. Think of her hearty laugh and her gentle caring ways."

The organ started a slow solemn melody as Esther began the long walk from her mother's side to the front of the church. She moved to her spot near the organ and waited.

The whole congregation watched as Esther closed her eyes to gather herself. She took a deep breath then nodded to the organist. Her beautiful copper skin and shoulder length, straight black hair, resembled her father. Proud, honest eyes and strong carved cheekbones came to life, as she opened her mouth and began to sing.

"Sweet is the promise- I will not forget thee," she sang with a voice so strong tht everybody said, "Amen".

"Nothing can molest or turn my soul away; E'em tho' the night be dark within the valley. Just beyond is shining one eternal day. I will not forget thee or leave thee," she sang, as her eyes blinked back tears. *"In My hands I'll hold thee, In My arms I'll fold thee; I will not forget thee or leave thee…"*
When she finished, she stood with her eyes closed. She paused for a moment to honor Ma Letty. Silence fell upon the church after the cacophony of Amens drifted away.

After Esther's song, everyone filed from the church with uplifted hearts. They left the way Ma Letty would have wanted. They rejoiced…

It was well into the night. It was a time when

Black-Eyed Peas and Cornbread

Eastend folks sat quietly in the cafe when there was no place else to go. The jukebox was playing. Music filled the room, but the café was quiet, as everyone drifted deeply into the core of their own souls.

Chapter 4

Looney looked at Mae Mae's face as she sat across from him in the dimly lit café. Though she was years older than he remembered, the face he saw was that of a young girl.

It wasn't the same girl who had climbed into his truck years before. Some things had changed but much more remained the same. There was one thing about her face that still had not changed. It still showed the suffering. It still showed the pain of years ago.

"There's so much I'm sorry for in my life, Looney," Mae Mae said with a deep sigh. "I done so much I can't even ask God for no more fo'giveness.

"When I met you on the road I thought God was settin' me free. I thought when I got in yo' truck an headed up that mountain I was bein' delivered from Hell. That's when you first took me to my Ma Letty…"

The house sat tucked between a church and a whorehouse. Five steep steps led from the alley beside the house up to the high front porch. A long dark hallway led from the porch to the heart of the house.

Two, one room dwellings on each side of the hallway stood facing each other, as if on guard. And straight ahead, waiting behind a glass curtained, wooden door, was Miss Letty.

The sound of laughter echoed loudly off the

walls as they approached the door. When they entered, Mae Mae's attention immediately turned to the large, dark laughing woman who lit up the room.

The woman was different from anyone Mae Mae had ever seen. She stood there heavy and smiling, like life was a wonderful adventure. When she laughed, her whole body laughed. Her big bright eyes lit up. And her face glowed like the morning sun.

Her free spirit was apparent by her ashy bare feet and her thinning blue dyed hair. A flowered dress that just barely fit over her wide hips and big stomach, shook when she laughed.

She glanced at Looney standing in the door with Mae Mae, but said nothing. She was busy selling a shot glass of corn liquor, humming a church hymn and telling her customer he'd better be in church on Sunday.

Her hands were on her hips when she turned and looked at them up then down. The expression on her face was like she already knew Mae Mae was coming.

"So, what kind of sad stories you got, lil' girl?" said Miss Letty. "I know there's some good reason for Looney to be standin' here wit' you."

"He brought me here, 'cause he thought you could help me," Mae Mae said shyly.

Miss Letty threw her head way back and laughed her loud hearty laugh. Everything in the junky, overfilled room shook when she laughed. It was the kind of laugh that made everyone listening want to laugh with her.

A. Jean Jackson

"Looney knows me like a book," she said. "He know good an well, any kind of stray he bring here, I ain't gone turn 'em away. You was sho' blessed runnin' into that one, girl."

"Yes mam. I could'na made it this far without him."

"Lets jus' say I was in da right place," Looney said, looking for a place to spit.

"So, what yo' name? An where you comin' from girl?" Miss Letty asked, smiling and patting Mae Mae on the hand.

"Mae Mae's my name. I'm from 'round Greenville. But I done ran away."

"You ran away! This here ain't no slavery times girl," Miss Letty said, laughing again.

"I had to," Mae Mae said through a flood of tears. "The man my mama sole me away to, I thought he was gone kill me."

"Yeah Letty, look at dat gals face where he done beat ha," said Looney. "Dat jus' don't make no sense. It 'bout broke my heart."

"Well honey, the Lord done sent you to the right place," said Miss Letty, with a look of pity. "I'm gone help you bes' I can."

"You won't be sorry you helped me," Mae Mae said.

"Jus settle down chile, every thang gone be a'right. Let me show you to a room. Then we can talk real good come mornin'."

Mae Mae hugged Looney, as she turned to leave. "Thank you," she said softly, as she looked deeply into his eyes. I ain't never gone forget what you done for me. Never."

A dust covered, creaky staircase led them to the rooms upstairs. Mae Mae walked slowly following Miss Letty until she stopped in front of a door at the top of the stairs.

When the door creaked open an old, musty smell greeted Mae Mae's nostrils. It was a good smell. It was like the smell was there because the room had been waiting. It had been waiting just for her.

"This a'right for you child?" Miss Letty asked.

"Sho', this real nice," Mae Mae said, looking around with a smile.

"Night then. See you in the mornin'," Miss Letty said as she departed.

The kerosene lamp on the table near the bed fluttered happily as the door closed. The faint light from it danced on the walls with her shadow. It directed her to the waiting bed.

Clean white sheets tucked neatly at the corners invited her inside the covers. She breathed in the newness, the peace, the safeness in the room as her head touched down on the pillow.

Sleep came swiftly. It was the first time in Mae Mae's life that the sleep she took was her own. It was the first time sleep truly belonged to her.

As she rose to her new world the following day, her old flowered wrap dress, with blood spots and rips from her ugly past, reminded her of the hell she'd left. She put it on and quickly went to the outhouse.

A. Jean Jackson

When she finished, she followed the sound of Miss Letty's voice and went back into the house. Eight strange men watched as she approached the table. Their eyes searched Mae Mae's young face as she served grits onto her plate. Everyone was quiet. They ate and they watched her.

"What you gone do today?" Miss Letty said, looking at Mae Mae and breaking the silence.

"I don't rightly know," Mae Mae replied, after a long pause.

"Well, can you cook?" she asked, laughing.

"Yes mam," said Mae Mae, full of pride. "I been cookin' since I was a little thing."

"You sure about that?"

"Oh yeah! I was the oldest girl. My mama use to make me cook for the whole family. An then if I didn't cook things jus' right for that man I was with, he'd sho' beat me good."

"Yeah, I guess you can cook, at that," Miss Letty said. "A'right then. I'm gone hire you to do the cookin' for this whole house. All these boarders gits they breatfas' an they gets suppa. You got to fix it, you got to serve it, an you got to clean up after.

"Do a good job, I'm gone give you spendin' change an yo' room an board. It's on trial basis tho'. I'm gone see what you do with suppa tonight."

"Thank you Lord!" Mae Mae said, as she put her hands together and looked up to the sky.

The frying pan sizzled with melted lard. Mae Mae put in a smooth pat of butter, and watched it disappear. The pan waited, as she smothered the chicken parts in a mixture of flour, salt and pepper. When she dropped a large breast into the pan, the loud crackling noise, told her the heat was just right.

All of the chicken was browned to a crispy perfection as she turned it over in the pan. The smell was dancing about the kitchen.

When the chicken was done, she took it out of the pan, and placed it neatly onto a large platter. Flour and water, poured into the still hot cast iron skillet, turned to a rich, brown gravy. As she stirred she smiled and inhaled the flavor.

Steam rose high into the air from the rice boiling in a large white pot. The smell of fresh collard greens circled and mingled with the others aromas.

Biscuits were taken from the oven with the end of her large apron. Placing them quickly on the table, she sighted Miss Letty entering the kitchen. "Well, lil' girl," she said, sniffing the air. "I see you wasn't lyin'. You can cook. Hope this stuff taste as good as it smell."

"It's gone be good," Mae Mae said.

Miss Letty rung the dinner bell and the men gathered. They gave thanks. Then, eating in silence, their eyes looked about with gracious satisfaction.

"Ya'll don't have to sit here all quiet," said Miss Letty. "I know everybody feelin' like strangers with the new girl here. But she ain't gone bite. The way ya'll gobblin' up that fried chicken I know you like her cookin'."

"Yeah! Yeah! We likes it real good," Howard

said, with the other men joining in.

"Where that gal come from anyhow?" asked Gerald, scratching the white fuzz on his round balding head.

"Now ya'll know I don't allow no meddlin' in folks' business when they live here," Miss Letty said firmly. If she tell you, that's her business.

Gerald looked down embarrassed, but his curiosity still showed in his eyes. "I sho' am glad she gone be cookin' for us," he said smiling, looking at Mae Mae with approval. "She almos' cook good as you do, Mizz Letty."

"I'm glad you said almos' boy," Miss Letty said laughing. "Now ya'll go on an relax on the front porch while I help this chile clean up. We'll be out there in a lil' bit."

Gerald, Howard and the other men migrated to the porch and sat way back in overstuffed pillow seats on the long high porch. As they picked their teeth, they were still savoring Mae Mae's meal.

After a short while in the kitchen, Mae Mae and Miss Letty ventured out to the porch. Miss Letty sat in a big wooden rocker that was placed at the center. It was there for her and only for her.

Mae Mae moved shyly to a distant corner of the porch. She sat in a swing in the dark; watching, listening, learning her new environment.

"How do, Corrine? An you, James?" Miss Letty shouted to two passers by, over the banister of the porch.

"How do?" Gerald shouted, with a big smile

covering his face.

Still smiling, Gerald waited for the couple to pass, then whispered loudly enough for everyone to hear. "Now that man know he need to go home to his wife."

"Hell, he be at that whore house every night," Howard shouted, as everyone erupted in laughter. "He mus' not be getting' none at home."

In the midst of the laughter, Miss Letty interrupted. "Now ya'll know I don't allow no talk like that," she said with a slight smile. "Them folks sho' don't need to be judged by ya'll. You don't know nothin' about what's in them people's souls. So jus' leave 'em be.

"They got to go right by that church before they go do whatever it is they do. God know what they doin'. They gone have to answer to him."

"Now you right 'bout that Mizz Letty," Gerald replied. He sighed and shifted thoughts. "It sho' is some kind of pretty out here on this porch. Look at all them stars lookin' down here at us."

"Yeah it remind me of them days on da farm with Mama and Daddy," said Miss Letty. "That was beautiful country. You could lay out in the middle of a fiel' an dream on the moon.

"An Daddy, he's jus' proud as he could be 'cause we wasn't no slaves. We didn't have a pot of our own to piss in, but we was free. That's all daddy cared about, that we was free."

"How you end up here, Mizz Letty?" Howard asked. "How you end up with this house. Ain't too many colored folks 'round here that own nothin'."

"It's a long story. You know how mos' ole ladies ain't got nothin' but stories. So when you ask, I sho' ain't gone do nothin' but tell you," she said, followed by her powerful laugh.

"Back when Daddy was share croppin' for a lil' food an a place to live, we was the only ones around there that was free. Daddy taught me that I ought to be real proud of that. To him, I was somebody special.

"He raised me like I didn't have to bow down to nobody. An honey, I acted like I was as good as anybody, even the white folks," she said with a smile, looking right at Mae Mae.

"Well, after I got to be 'bout sixteen I started goin' to work at the white folks house, right along beside Mama. Lord! Honey! I was up in there thankin' that white woman was supposed to work for me. To them folks we worked for, I was a uppity nigga.

"So after a while Mama found out about this Quaker woman that was wantin' to teach a colored girl school lessons in exchange for work. Well, I turned out to be that girl.

"This white lady was named Mizz Logan. I ain't never gone forget her. She live right here in Asheville right now. She took me in an taught me a lil' readin' an writin' jus' like she promised. She wasn't like most whites. She didn't walk around actin' like the queen of the big house.

"Lord! I remember I used to love lookin' at this big ole globe in her house. She had some real fine thangs. But that globe with all the countries in the worl' on it, was really somethin'.

"I didn't mind cookin' an cleanin' up for her. 'Cause I knew Mizz Logan wasn't askin' me 'cause I was colored. Bless her heart, she be cleanin' an sweatin' right there beside me most times.

"She gave me somethin' worth more than anything I ever got in my whole life. That readin', writin' and lil' bit of figurin' gone be with me 'til I die. Can't nobody never take that from me.

"Mizz Logan was the perfect example of a God fearin' woman. She wasn't jus' makin' out like she love God. That lady was livin' it. She was like that when most white folks didn't care what happened to coloreds.

"I lived with Mizz Logan for a few years. Then after a time I had a yearnin' to go out on my own. So one day I packed my few belongins', and started out the door to try out life for myself.

"Before I could get out the door, she reached in this vase on top of the piano an pulled out a roll of money. She put that money in my hand an hugged me for a long time.

"I walked away from her house an ended up right here in Eastend. An I ain't never left," she said, looking to the sky reverently.

"Yeah, but how you git this house?" Gerald asked, as everyone else appeared mesmerized by her story.

"Well, with the lil' bit of money I saved, an the money she gave me, I rented me a room right here in this house. A white man name o' Mr. Cooper used to come down here rentin' out dese rooms to the colored folks.

"So I asked him why he don't jus' let me run this house. I told him I could collect the rent money an take care of this place real nice. Ain't no white man never wanted to come to Eastend no way. So he let me start bein' the landlord.

"After jus' a few years I had all kinds of money. I was savin' up every penny I got. I was collectin' a little extra for changin' sheets an doin' folk's laundry. I was even sellin' a little corn liquor by the shot glass, on the side.

"Pretty soon, I was talkin' to Mr. Cooper, about buyin' this place for myself. To this day, he still wonderin' where in the worl' I got enough money to buy this place.

"I wasn't gone work myself to death in some white folks house, bein' no maid. My poor mama wasn't never able to do nothin' else. She died without havin' nothin' to show for bein' in this worl'. I ain't never wanted to spend my life slavin' for other folk's dreams."

Mae Mae was in awe as she hid behind the darkness that had fallen on the porch. "I don't know Mizz Letty that well," she thought to herself. "But I sho' do wish I could be jus' like her."

The quickly cooling night mountain air brought about a slow retreat. One by one they rose from deep inside their cushioned chairs and said goodnight.

Mae Mae struggled up the stairs in the

darkness. The unfamiliar steepness caused her to walk with caution. She felt her way holding on to the banister. When she finally reached the top she breathed a sigh of relief.

The room opened up to Mae Mae and she walked inside. It was really hers. It belonged to her. It made her feel like she was a real person.

The rusty water stain right in the middle of the ceiling caught her eye as she laid on the bed. It was the last thing she saw before she drifted off deeply into her dreams.

Now she believed it was alright for a colored woman to have dreams. She believed it was alright to want to be somebody.

Chapter 5

Fall was slowly dwindling away. But the sun glared down refusing to leave without a fight. Mae Mae shielded her eyes with her hands. She looked up to the sky, pleased that the dreadful winter cold of the Asheville Mountains had not yet arrived.

Padgitt's store was much further than she thought. But there was no turning back, as she walked faster, determined to get there and back before dark.

For a brief moment, she stopped to catch her breath, taking the opportunity to look about at the buildings and houses. People of all shades of brown and black moved about and stood around the bustling Eagle Street as she passed. Others stood around making deals and playing numbers secretly yet everyone knew. All of the action, all of the movement, let her know how different this place was from the spread out rural life at Red's and Cora Lee's.

"You can't come in this front do'," a voice shouted from behind the counter.

"Yessir," Mae Mae said, embarrassed. "Sorry sir. I ain't never been here before."

"Well, niggas uses the back do'. The sooner you learns that, the better. Now what is it you needin'."

"Sir, I know I got to get some eggs. The rest on this list right here. I can't make out what it say though."

Black-Eyed Peas and Cornbread

Padgitt grabbed the paper out of her hand and looked at it. Dust flew as he marched angrily about the store. She watched closely as he searched the shelves, dodging the big cloth bags stacked on the dirty wooden floor.

The black stove in the middle of the floor sat cold and idle. It stood big and tall like it was the one in charge. It watched her like it was daring her to move.

"Damn stupid ass niggas," Padgitt said, as he placed a box of baking soda on the counter. "I ain't never in my life seed such a stupid good for nothin' group of people. Every damn day of my life I got to do every thang. I got to read for 'em. I got to count change for 'em. If I lived with 'em, I'd probably have ta wipe they butts."

Mae Mae looked down as she handed him money. He snatched the single bill out of her hand and slammed the change down on the counter.

"Here! Now gone an git' out of my damn face," he said.

Mae Mae departed through the back door, still looking down. Once she was out of the door, she breathed. For the first time since she entered Padgitt's world, she was really able to breath.

She was glad to be in the alley outside. The dust and the stench of rotten discarded food in the back of the store was better than what she'd experienced inside.

On the walk back home she saw nothing. The sick feeling in her stomach was holding her brain captive. The sinking feeling in her soul immobilized her senses. The only thing she could make out was how to get home.

Large drops of rain spattered on the dusty road, as the sun still shined above her head. And for once, she was thankful for the rain. The rain cleansed and renewed her. The wet warmth of it made her feel less like a dirty, stupid, good for nothing nigger.

"Come on in here gal, an git out of them wet clothes, Mae Mae," Miss Letty shouted.

Miss Letty watched as the rains poured down heavier and heavier as Mae Mae ran past her on the porch. "Wonda what's wrong with her," she said, mumbling to herself.

The look of despair on Mae Mae's face so concerned the older woman that slowly, at her own pace, she climbed the steps one by one. The sturdy wooden rail on the left side of the stairs carried her to the top. Before she reached the door she paused to gather her thoughts.

"Hey gal, you in there," Miss Letty shouted through the door.

"Yes mam," Mae Mae yelled back, slowly opening the door.

"OK Chile. What on earth's the matter with you. You ain't been right since you got back from that store. Now tell me what happened!"

"I don't know," Mae Mae said, looking down at the floor. "I keep thinkin' I ain't never gone be nobody. Red was always beatin' me down. Then soon as I start to thankin' things gittin' better, that white man at the store treat me like a dog.

Black-Eyed Peas and Cornbread

"Mizz Letty, I know he ain't no different from most white folks. They treat coloreds like we still slaves. To most of them we ain't even human."

"OK! What else's new. That ain't changin' no time soon," said Miss Letty.

"So I guess you sayin' why I got to be so hurt by all this? 'Cause I can't read, that's why. I can't help it if I can't read an write. I could learn things, if I jus' had the chance," she shouted, with tears in her eyes.

"Oh!" Miss Letty said, with a slight smile forming on her face. "That's what this all about. What that evil man say to you chile?"

"He jus' made a big thing out of havin' to read that list for me. That don't make me stupid. Do it Mizz Letty?"

"No chile. That don't make you stupid. Sometime white folks don't care what's in colored folks heads. Jus' like most don't stop hatin' us long enough to see what's in our hearts either."

"But the thing you got to remember in this life, is you can't be judgin' yo'self on what other folks be sayin'."

"I found out a long time ago honey. Can't nobody hold you back but yo' own self. You got to think in yo' own heart that you is somebody."

Miss Letty's words flooded from her mouth as if she'd been waiting to speak them for a long time. Her words came forth like they had been there all along, just waiting to be shared with Mae Mae.

"Chile that's somethin' can't nobody take from you. No matter what happen or how low you made to

A. Jean Jackson

feel, if you think you somebody special, then you is. You understand what I'm sayin' to you."

"Yes mam. Yes mam, I think I do. But you know what. I would still think a heap more of myself if I could read. You think you can teach me?"

"Sweetie, I don't know nothin' 'bout teachin' nobody that stuff. I can read a lil'. I know my name when I see it wrote down. An I can figure enough to git by. But I can't teach nobody nothin'."

"Oh!" Mae Mae said, disappointed.

"But I tell you what. Since this mean so much to you. I'm gone go see Miss Logan. Maybe she won't mind teachin' you some.

"Thank you Mizz Letty. Thank you for carin' about me."

They left together, with one supporting the other as they struggled down the poorly lit stairs. On their way to the kitchen, both of them carried a renewed spirit.

"God! It's rainin' out there like it ain't never gone stop, Howard said, sitting down at the table.

"You mean it ain't stopped yet?" asked Miss Letty.

"Sho' ain't," Gerald said, butting in. "They sayin' at the railroad yard it's gone flood bad. An we all know what that mean."

"What?" asked Mae Mae, thinking she was the only one in the room who didn't know.

"Las' time it rained like dis," Gerald said. "Everything in this town stopped. Nobody wasn't gittin' in an nobody wasn't gittin' out. It was hard times for everybody.

They all gathered for dinner, clouded by a general mood of despair. "Lord!" Miss Letty said, praying with a loud energy. "Help us to see yo' plan. We jus' yo' lowly servants put here on this earth for reasons only you know. We could be getting' ready to have some real hard times now. But help us to see how blessed we is.

"You done gave us this food. An you done gave us each other. We pray for dry skies, and we pray for the special need hangin' on Mae Mae's heart. Thank you Lord. Amen!"

"Amen!" Gerald shouted, as everyone else at the table chimed in.

For days Mae Mae heard the familiar sound of rain pounding on the roof of the house. It was the same rhythmic sound that always soothed her when she was growing up in Cora Lee's house. But now, in this place and in this time, she prayed for it to end.

"I know this may be selfish Lord. But the sooner this storm let up, then Mizz Letty can talk to that Mizz Logan about learnin' me some things.

"God! I got these feelings in my heart that you mean for me to be somebody. But seem like something always standin' in my way, Lord. Please, jus' keep on helpin' me see yo' way."

It seemed that the rains would continue forever. Falling steadily for a week then off and on for days, the rain and the constant clouds blocked the sun like holding it prisoner.

A. Jean Jackson

The time, the long moments of immobilization gave them time to think, time to catch up with their inner selves. It was a time that changed Mae Mae. It was a time where though she or noone else would really ever know, she became a woman.

And then, just as suddenly as the floods came, they were gone. They cleansed the earth. And then they were gone.

"I got a present for you, gal," said Miss Letty, days after the rains finally let up.

"What is it? What is it?" Mae Mae asked, excitedly.

"I went to see Mizz Logan today. Honey I ain't seen her in years. She hugged me like I was long los' family. We sat an talked for a long time. She say she been ailin' some. But she got a older sister livin' with her now that's worse off than her.

"I tol' her about you," Miss Letty continued, smiling. "I asked her if she think she might can teach you some."

"What she say? What she say?" Mae Mae exclaimed, unable to contain her excitement.

"She said if you come by in the mornin', she'll talk with you about it. She sayin' she weak an ole. But anybody wantin' to learn that bad, she gone help all she can."

The walk from Eastend into the prosperity of Montford Avenue intensified Mae Mae's fear as she approached the large white house. She breathed a sigh before knocking. She smoothed her clothes and her hair. And wiped the mud from her shoes.

She knocked and then she waited. A grey haired, light skinned colored woman with her hands on her hips, opened the door and looked at Mae Mae. "You 'spose to go to da back do'," she said, looking at Mae Mae through small wire rim bifocals. Where in da worl' you comin' from you don't know dat?"

"I'm here to see Mizz Logan, mam," Mae Mae said, looking past the woman into the house. 'Mizz Logan tol' me to come. She gone be teachin' me some readin'."

"Yeah, well dats fine. But you still needs to go right back out dere to da side o' da house, an in through the kitchen. Go on now!"

As she made her way to the back of the house, Mae Mae could hear the woman talking under her breath. "All dese niggas jus' dyin' ta know readin' and writin'. Why dey thank dey got ta do dat anyhow. What on earf dey gone use it fa."

Mae Mae entered as the woman directed her inside. "I'm gone let Mizz Logan know you here," she said, pointing to a chair at the table. "Sit here 'til I git back. Don't move. An don't you dare touch nothin'."

Mae Mae watched as the old woman, dressed in a freshly starched white apron, disappeared from the room. She waited, glued to the chair just as she had been directed.

The brightness of the clean white walls surrounded Mae Mae, pleasantly blinding her like fresh fallen snow. The shiny floors, the abundance of windows, the bold expensive furniture, the china, the silver, the riches overwhelmed her.

"Come on dis way. Mizz Logan waitin' in da parlor," the colored woman said, when she reappeared.

She led Mae Mae through a dark hall that wound around past a shiny polished stairway. The towering wooden door stood majestically at the front of the house. It was the door Mae Mae had not been allowed to enter. Though now she walked right by it in route to the parlor.

The parlor sat to the right of the staircase. Upon entering, it struck her that everything throughout the house had an old, dark mahogany elegance. Books circled the room on immaculately stacked shelves. And in the corner, close to a large window, the magnificent globe Miss Letty had spoken of was still there.

The old white woman sat quietly waiting. Her sparkling blue eyes surrounded by a crown of thinning but beautiful snow-white hair, welcomed Mae Mae. A wrinkled hand clutching a dark brown oak cane decorated in brass, balanced her as she reached the other hand to Mae Mae.

"My dear," she said, smiling. "I am Miss Logan. Letty told me all about you. She said you want to learn to read."

"Ah, yes mam," Mae Mae said, feeling stupid and trying not to stutter.

"Well Dear, I think I can help with that. How long have you been in Asheville, living with Letty?"

"I ain't been here all that long. Jus' a few

months now, mam.

"Tell me Dear, why is learning so important to you?"

"Mam, I don't rightly know for sho'. All I know is, I jus' want to be somebody. I know my head be jus' poundin' sometime, wantin' to know more things. It hurt me when I get treated stupid, when I know I ain't. I want to jus' have the chance. Then if I can't do it, at least I tried."

"I see," Miss Logan said, pleased with the answer. "How soon shall we start?"

"I'm ready," Mae Mae said, bursting with excitement.

"Tell you what, Dear. Come tomorrow as early as you can get here.

"Viola!" she called to the old colored lady. "Would you kindly show Mae Mae the way out please. Mae Mae, I take it you've met Viola. I've been trying to get her to get interested in learning. She's been with us for years and just refuses to even try."

"Mizz Logan," Viola said with a fake smile, "Ain't none o' dat learnin' gone help me clean dis' here house no betta. I keep tellin' you dat. Learnin' fa dese young folks.

"Come on gal if you want me ta sho' ya out. I got plenty o' work I need ta be doin'."

They left Miss Logan standing in the warmth of the sun pouring in through the large window. Mae Mae followed as Viola led her through the long dark hall leading to the kitchen. Viola held the back door open for Mae Mae to leave.

A. Jean Jackson

"When you come back, you better know how to act in white folk's houses," Viola said. "I seed you sittin' up in dat parlor actin' like you special. Mizz Logan, she nice. But you better not be actin' like dat 'round Mizz Sneed. Mizz Logan's sista don't take ta niggas like she do."

Mae Mae left with the warning ringing in her ears. But she refused to let Viola spoil her excitement. No matter what it took, she was determined to learn as much as she could.

The walk home that day and all of the routine duties she carried out in Miss Letty's kitchen became a part of her path to true freedom. To her, freedom was being somebody. And being somebody had everything to do with knowledge.

Later that night as she slept, her dreams were bright and calm and free. She was able to feel in her dream, the cushioned softness of perfectly green grass. It caressed her bare feet as she walked towards the rising sun.

A light breeze lifted her dark flowing hair. It revealed skin as smooth and radiant as a new spring day. It revealed to Mae Mae her own likeness, her own face. And in that face she saw for the first time ever, a woman.

The next morning Mae Mae was forced to awake early. She held on tightly to the railing as she ran down the steps. And once on the porch, she ran frantically to the outhouse.

"This' place smell bad, jus' like it always do," she said to herself. "But it ain't never made me throw up like this. God! I jus' don't feel good."

She went back to the house holding her stomach. Dizziness and the bad taste in her mouth went with her. The aroma of country ham, scrambled eggs and grits brought back her nausea as she entered the kitchen. She forced herself to continue the cooking Miss Letty had begun.

"What's wrong gal," Miss Letty said. "Look like you turnin' pale. Dark as you is, somethin' must be awful wrong."

"I don't know Mizz Letty," Mae Mae said, looking for a place to sit down. "I ain't been feelin' all that good for a few days now. Then this mornin' I ran straight to the outhouse an threw up. I ain't never felt like this before."

Miss Letty sat down beside her with a half smile on her face. She took Mae Mae's chin in her hands and turned her head from side to side. The smile on Miss Letty's face grew larger as she searched deeply into Mae Mae's eyes. She looked at the pulse in Mae Mae's neck and then sat way back in her chair.

"Chile, look like to me you pregnant."

"Oh God! No! please no!"

"Honey, that's somethin' you ought to be rejoicin' about. Havin' a baby is a gift from God."

"I know but. But…"

"But what lil' girl? Let me tell you somethin' Mae Mae. You ain't been livin' here but a few months. For most folks that ain't no long time. But in that lil' bit of time, you already like my own chile. Everybody

A. Jean Jackson

here care a lot about you. Whatever you worried about, jus' go ahead an tell me."

"Mizz letty, I don't know whose baby this is."

"It ain't that man's who you ran away from? It got to be his. You ain't been with nobody else?"

"Well, mam I kinda was! There was a man named Jacob back where I came from. Lord, I loved that man with all my heart. That short time I had with him was the happiest days of my life."

"One day Red caught us together. With one look at us together, he could tell how much I loved Jacob. And he couldn't stand it. The day I ran off an left that place, was the day Red killed Jacob.

"Mizz Letty," she said with tears in her eyes. "I ain't never gone forget the sound of that gun goin' off in my ears. I ain't never told another soul about it but you."

"Oh *chile!*" Miss Letty said, wrapping her arms around Mae Mae's shoulders. "You've shouldered more of a load than any of God's children should have to. You mean this baby could be Jacob's or it could be Red's?"

"Yeah. I 'spose, that's what it mean. An I'm scared, Miss Letty. I'm scared that if it turn out to be Red's, I ain't gone love it the same. I hate feelin' like that about my own flesh an blood."

"Far as I'm concerned you feel the same as anybody who been through what you have. But we gone love that baby. Don't matter whose it is. We gone love that chile jus' like we love you. Remember that, you hear, chile?"

Black-Eyed Peas and Cornbread

"Now, if you feelin' some better, you got some schoolin' to do today. You feel up to goin'?"

"Can't nothin' in this world stop me from that," Mae Mae said smiling proudly.

"By the way, I got somethin' for you," Miss Letty said, handing Mae Mae a book. This here is what Mizz Logan give to me all them years ago. I want you to have it now. Soon as you able to read it, let me know. Since my ole eyes done got so bad, you gone be able to read it for me."

"What book is it, Mizz Letty?"

"Uncle Tom's Cabin."

Mae Mae was like a little girl. Her excitement showed in her smile as she walked out the door passed the church. The walk through Eastend to Montford Avenue was different this time. This time, she was a mature woman on her way to making a better life for herself and her child. The sun shown brighter than ever, the sky was as blue as she had ever seen it.

Having learned her first lesson from Viola, she went directly to the back door. Viola greeted her in the usual non-chalant manner. Mumbling the whole way, she escorted Mae Mae to the parlor. While Mae Mae waited, she watched the sunlight play with the colors of the twirling globe. A smile crossed her face as she thought of Miss Letty.

"One of these days, thanks to Mizz Letty, I'm gone be able to look at this globe and know how to find where I am," she said to herself. "All these shapes and colors mean somethin'. I don't know what they mean. But this sho' is a pretty thang."

"Don't you dare touch that!" a voice shouted from the door. "Who are you anyway, girl?"

Miss Logan's soothing voice cut in as she entered the room in time to rescue Mae Mae. "Oh, Mae Mae, Dear. Meet my sister Miss Sneed. Jenny this is Mae Mae. She's going to be my student."

"Your student! Elynor, my God! When are you going to learn? Colored folks don't have minds for learning. It's a waste. It's a damn waste of your time, Elynor."

"I know Jenny," Miss Logan said, winking at Mae Mae. "But we're going to give it a try anyway."

"Well, she better know her place. I don't want her in here touching and handling everything."

"Mae Mae did you hear that?" asked Miss Logan, with the same calm voice as always. "My sister would feel better if you wouldn't touch things."

Satisfied for the moment, Miss Sneed with her plump red cheeks, and heavy hips waddled slowly out of the room. Miss Logan and Mae Mae watched her disappear into the darkness of the hall.

"Mae Mae please understand," Miss Logan said, when they were alone. "My sister and I feel quite differently about most things concerning Negroes. She's old and weak. And many times I lead her to believe that she's the one in charge. It makes her feel better.

"But remember Mae Mae, in this room I want you to feel free to relax. I want you to feel comfortable. I want you to feel completely free to learn. Don't worry about her, do you hear? She's harmless. Now! What were you touching that so upset Jenny?"

"That globe over yonder by the window," Mae Mae said with a weak smile. "I was thinkin' how maybe one day I might could find where I live on there."

"Well Dear, why don't we make that our first lesson."

They walked together towards the window. The sun still showing its morning brightness, smiled down on them as the shiny sphere twirled with Miss Logan's touch.

When it stopped, she pointed. "You are here Dear. This is western North Carolina. Asheville is not actually written on this globe. But if it were, it would be right here."

Mae Mae smiled broadly as if she had just discovered America. A tremendous lust for learning showed in her eyes. It was a look that Miss Logan had not seen for a very long time.

Chapter 6

The heat of the summer in Eastend in was just like all of Asheville in 1925. It seemed unusually unbearable for everyone, but especially for Mae Mae. It added to Mae Mae's misery as she walked to Miss Logan's house. The extra effort she was forced to exert because of her pregnancy, was a constant reminder of her discontent.

The whole ordeal had haunted her for months. Each day, with every inch of flesh developing in her womb, it became more difficult to love the mystery growing inside of her. Now with a swollen belly, the mixed emotions floating around in her heart were impossible to ignore.

"What's wrong with you, Gal?" Padgitt said, as Mae Mae walked past his store. "Look like yo' ass all blowed up," he said, laughing along with the other men sitting on the outside of the store.

"That's the one thang about you colored gals. Ya'll have babies faster than a rabbit in heat."

Mae Mae kept walking trying to ignore the thunder of laughter. "I hate that man," she said, under her breath. "One of these days I'm gone show him."

The echo of the men's laughter stayed in her ears all the way to Montford Avenue. By the time she reached Miss Logan's house, she was more determined than ever to have a good lesson.

When Miss Logan entered the room and their lesson began, Mae Mae formed the letters M-A-E M-A-E R-E-D-M-A-N at the top of her paper. Miss Logan watched patiently as the slender fingers of Mae Mae's left hand moved gracefully over the page.

"That's very good Mae Mae," said Miss Logan. "Now write the whole alphabet just like I showed you before. Write them all in capitals and then write the lower case letters. Take your time. I'll be back to check on you in a moment."

Mae Mae licked the end of her pencil and turned her full attention to writing as Miss Logan eased out of the door. Slowly, carefully she wrote A-B-C-D. Then suddenly she paused as a mild cramping sensation moved from the small of her back to the center of her stomach.

Moments later the cramps turned into a sharp pain. Mae Mae closed her eyes and began to rub her stomach. When the pains got stronger she grabbed the side of the chair. "God! I hope this baby ain't comin' now," she said to herself.

She prayed that the pains would go away. But by the time Miss Logan returned to the room, Mae Mae was clinching her teeth and clutching her swollen belly. The pain was almost unbearable.

"Mae Mae, Dear are you alright?" Miss Logan asked, alarmed by the look of fear and pain on Mae Mae's face.

"Yes mam," Mae Mae answered, trying to sit up straight, trying to pretend the pains weren't there. "I think I ought to be leavin' though. I don't want to take no chances on this baby comin' right here."

"Certainly Dear," said Miss Logan. "Do you need Viola to help you home?"

A. Jean Jackson

"No mam. I think I can make it," Mae Mae said, forcing herself to get to her feet.

Viola sat at the kitchen table peeling potatoes, watching as Mae Mae approached the back door. "Um! Um! Um!" Viola grunted, before Mae Mae could reach for the knob. "Look like you gone have that baby any day. You big as a horse. Why you still tryin' to come here lookin' like that. Learnin' ain't worth all that is it?"

"Yes mam," said Mae Mae. "It sho' is. I'm gone be comin' here 'til I can't move no more," she said., rushing through the door.

"Well like I said before," Viola mumbled, as if Mae Mae were still standing there. "I don't see no reason for all this learnin'. You still gone have to be somebodies' maid, jus' like me."

Miss Letty's house seemed farther away today than ever. But Mae Mae was determined to get home. She rushed through the streets of Eastend almost in a daze. When she finally arrived home, she struggled up the stairs to the safety of her bed.

She fell onto the bed searching out its warmth and familiarity. The bed took on the form of her body, shaped by months of holding only her. It sunk in the middle to her weight, as always. And as always, it made her feel better.

The cramps eased and Mae Mae's afternoon sleep came easier. It captured her body serving as an ali to the miserable heat. It became a brief escape from all that tormented her soul. But from the child growing inside of her, taking over her body without her permission, escape had become impossible.

After a long nap she stood as her tall rounding frame took over the mirror in front of her. "Lord! I look jus' like Cora Lee with this big ole belly," Mae Mae said.

"I remember when Cora Lee was expectin'. She was always in a bad mood. She was already ugly, an her fat round face made her look jus' like a big hog.

"She was always cussin'. That's what I remember most about her. I think I heard that woman cussin' the day I was born.

"My daddy use to come an go like he wanted to. An Cora Lee really hated that. But when he came to the house, she was still in there doin' it with him. An pretty soon he'd leave an she'd end up havin' another baby.

"I think that's why Cora Lee stayed so mad an evil. She was givin' so much an havin' all them children, an him or nobody else wasn't never givin' nothin' back to her.

"I'm scared to have this baby. I seen Cora Lee have em'. But I ain't never had none myself. Cora Lee didn't never look scared. She was too mean to be scared.

"Cora Lee didn't seem to mind pain either. I think she enjoyed seein' other folk's pain. Like when she use to make me braid my sister's hair jus' because she knew it was gone hurt. She'd say, Mae Mae git over there an comb out Suga's hair." An she knew how tender headed Suga was.

A. Jean Jackson

"I'd be hatin' every minute of it. I wasn't never intendin' to hurt Suga none. But sometime I be so mad at Cora Lee, I would comb out Suga's kinky hair jus' like I didn't care.

"Suga be cryin' the whole time. An I be combin' out them naps right at the back of her head, wishin' it was Cora Lee."

"Cora Lee was a evil person. She wasn't no better than Red. Both of them was jus' like the devil. I jus' pray that this baby ain't nothin' like neither one of them."

She squinted at her pregnant image in the mirror, trying to block out thoughts of Cora Lee. For a moment, the image in the mirror was Cora Lee. It was an image that Mae would never forget. It was an image she would always hate. And for that very moment she hated any part of Cora Lee that had been forced on her.

That night the coolness of the air briefly visiting the porch was a welcome change from the heat of the day. The stars shined brightly to the backdrop of a perfectly blue sky. A crescent moon with a lone star sitting at its foot, sat majestically above them looking down. It seized the opportunity to brag of its beauty. The calmness, the peacefulness was overwhelming.

"Look at that moon," Miss Letty said, as everyone departed leaving she and Mae Mae alone. After a moment of silence, Miss Letty sighed. "How you really doin' Chile?" she said with a look of concern capturing her face.

"Mizz Letty, I suppose I'm alright. I was havin'

some pains today when I was at Mizz Logan's. I don't know what it mean though."

"Don't worry about that Chile. That baby jus' lettin' you know it ain't gone be long."

"I know one thing," Mae Mae said. "God must got a reason for makin' women folk carry babies this long. After somethin' growin' in you, right next to yo' heart this long, it's hard not feelin' somethin'. I know my mama ain't felt nothin' for none of her children. God I hope I don't end up treatin' mine like she did."

"I try real hard to get ready for whatever this baby gone be. Every time it move inside me, a good feelin' go right through me. It even make me smile sometime. Then by the time I get to feelin' half way good, I get this big picture of Red in my head.

"That's when the hate start goin' all through me. That's when I try my best to hate this chile. 'Cause you jus' don't know, Miss Letty. Ain't no way you can even imagine how much I hate that man."

"I ain't never felt that kind of hate for nobody," Miss Letty said. "But the hate you got ain't doin' nothin' but takin' you further and further from God. You got to let some of that go Chile. You can't let them feelins' keep you from God."

"You know what? I ain't seen you go to church the whole time you been here. I ain't never said nothin' cause really it ain't none of my business. But now, you like my own chile."

"So anyway, two things gone change around here real soon. One is you gone start callin' me Ma Letty. The other is, when the church doors open up tomorrow, I want you sittin' right beside me."

"Now ain't no reason for you thankin' you in this worl' all by yourself. When you got me an God on yo' side, life can't be no better."

Mae Mae rose slowly to return to her room. But she moved with a renewed energy. The steps leading to her room awaited her. But this time as she climbed them, they weren' as step. A great burden seemed to be lifted. This time she took them one at a time reaching the top without rest, without hesitation.

Inside the room, she smiled at the bed still holding her shape from her afternoon nap. Undressing, exposing all of the new rolls of fat that had formed around her midsection, she placed herself inside the waiting contours of the bed. Thoughts of the last time she went to church raced on in her mind…

Smiles seldom seen, like clouds blocking a sun too bashful to show itself, magically appeared on Sundays. As their feet touched the dirt road leading away from Cora Lee, each one of the children changed. Somehow personalities hidden deep inside, came to life on the road leading to church.

"I thank I'm gone do it today," Mae Mae said, blushing.

"What you talkin' 'bout girl," Suga fired back.

"You know! I told you Robert been askin' me for a kiss. An I done made up my mind. Today I'm gone do it. A lil' kiss ain't never hurt nothing."

"Only thing I got to say about it. You better not

never let Cora Lee fin' out. No tellin' what she'll do."

"Well, at least I be dyin' happy. 'Cause I'm gone kiss that pretty nigga today," Mae Mae said, as they both laughed. They skipped the final distance to the church.

During the service, eyes that saw his every move yet avoided his stare, looked across the aisle. Her hands shook. Her heart beat rapidly. Her palms were wet. Her stomach churned with fear and excitement.

Outside after the service Robert came to her. Long legs and muscular arms came towards her with a confidence that showed in his movement. His smile gleamed in the sun, as straight, white teeth, covered by full plump lips, teased her.

"Hey Mae Mae," he said. "Well, you gone do it?"

"I guess," she said shyly. "Where 'bouts?"

"Come on this way," he said, taking her by the hand.

She followed him deeply into the woods as they walked on a worn path. They walked past a row of tall oaks toward a grassy glade. When he reached the tree on the other side with the freshly carved heart, he stopped.

They looked at each other, and he pulled her close. He grabbed hold and held her so tightly that she couldn't breath. His soft wet tongue searched out hers, piercing deeply into her mouth.

When she was finally able to push him away and catch her breath, she wiped off her mouth

A. Jean Jackson

wanting no part of it. He rolled over and moved back towards her. "What's wrong?" he said, breathing heavily.

"I was gone kiss you. I jus' don't want to do nothin' else," she said. "I ain't never done that before."

"It's not gone hurt, Mae Mae. Come on please. Please!" he begged, over powering her, tearing at her dress.

"Stop!" she yelled loudly, getting up, brushing off. "I said no!"

"OK! OK! Jus' promise you won't tell. I won't do it no mo', OK."

Mae Mae said nothing. She ran through the woods back to the road to her waiting brothers and sisters.

"Yo' dress all tore up Mae Mae, what in the worl' happened?" Suga asked. "That boy try to take more than a kiss?"

"Yeah! What I'm gone tell Cora Lee. She gone know somethin' happened when she see this dress."

"I'm gone try to walk close to you," Suga said, planning nervously. "We all gone jus' stay between you an Cora Lee. That way you can go put somethin' else on before she see it."

Five of Cora Lee's children entered the door cautiously. They all surrounded Mae Mae. Cora Lee looked up as the big black mole in the center of her forehead appeared like a third eye.

"What ya'lls asses lookin' like a bunch of baby chicks for," she said. "Come here Mae Mae. Hand me that fly swatter over there."

"I'll get it for you," Suga said, diving to reach for it in the corner.

"Since when yo' lazy ass wantin' to do somethin'," Cora Lee said to Suga.

"What ya'll tryin' to hide anyway. You know you can't hide nothin' from me. Now get yo' ass over here Mae Mae."

Mae Mae moved slowly towards Cora Lee. She tried her best to cover the tear in her dress. Tears formed in her eyes and fell on the table in front of her.

"Yeah! I figured somethin' wasn't right. Look at yo' dress Gal. What happened to yo' black ass? Seem like you could go someplace like church, an stay out of trouble."

"Nothin'," Mae Mae said, lookin' down.

"Come here, Lil' Man," Cora Lee shouted to the middle boy, "Now you tell me what went on at that church or I'm gone make you wish you did."

"I don't know," Lil' Man said, through tears of his own.

"Well you take yo'self out side and cut wood. Don't you stop. An don't you let me see yo' ass res'. You keep choppin' til somebody tell me somethin'. Go on now!"

Lil' Man walked outside to the woodpile as Mae Mae and Suga glanced at each other. By the time bedtime arrived the steady sound of chopping still echoed on the outside of the house. An Mae Mae could stand the sound no longer.

Cora Lee was still sitting where they had found her after church, as Mae Mae approached. She sat

A. Jean Jackson

comfortable and cozy like the queen as the steady sounds of torture coming from the outside did not seem to affect her.

"Mama," Mae Mae said, nervously. "I got somethin' to tell you."

"Yeah! It's about time. I thought you was gone let yo' brotha chop up a whole tree before you said somethin'. Now what in the hell went on at that church today?"

"Well," Mae Mae said, looking down at the floor. "I went to the woods with this boy. But I jus' tol' him he could kiss me. So we was kissin' an then he tried to get me on the ground. I was fightin' tryin' to get up. 'Cause I wasn't gone do nothin' else. An that's' when he tore my dress."

"Well, well, well," Cora Lee said, shaking her head from side to side. "What was yo' fas' ass doin' in the woods in the firs' place. You know these boys ain't out for nothin' but some pussy. What make you thank you so special all they want is a kiss from yo' black ass."

"I tell you what. You big an bad enough to be trapsin' off to the woods with these boys. I got somethin' that gone fix yo' lil' fas' ass. Now get on out there an get yo' brother."

The cruel punishment that Cora Lee intended for Mae Mae was to sell her off to Red. It was one of many horrible realities that came back to her disguised as dreams as she drifted off to sleep…

"You 'bout ready?" Shouted Miss Letty through

Black-Eyed Peas and Cornbread

Mae Mae's door. "Come on now. I ain't never late goin' to the house of the Lord."

"Ma Letty, um, I ain't got nothin' really to wear to church. I been lookin' at these few lil' dresses I got, an don't none fit that good."

"Chile the Lord don't pay no mind to what folks got on. He jus' glad you care enough to come. Come on down these steps. Maybe big as I am, you can wear somethin' I got over that big belly."

When they reached her room, Ma Letty reached into a small curtained closet. She pulled out a large blue and gold print dress and handed it to Mae Mae. "Here, see if this'll fit you," Ma Letty said, sounding as if she intended for it to fit all along. "Seem like without the belt it ought to fit fine."

Mae Mae reached for it shyly and looked around for a place to change. "Look gal, yo about to make me late," Miss Letty said fussing playfully. "Gone right over there by the bed an get that dress on."

Mae Mae moved a few steps to the other side of the room. She stood at the foot of the large mahogany bed, as if it would shield her. She glanced quickly at Ma Letty then tried to pull it over her head.

The dress fit so snugly that both of them had to work together to get it over Mae Mae's stomach. She shifted the waistline back and forth until she was satisfied, then looked in the mirror and smiled.

"Now try this," Ma Letty said, handing Mae Mae a flowery straw dress hat. "This here what make a girl a 'real lady'."

A. Jean Jackson

They walked together arm in arm to the church. With heads held high, adorned with fancy little hats and delicate nets covering their faces, they entered the church doors.

"Ladies an gentleman, welcome to the house of the Lord," a big voice sounded from the pulpit. "I feels extra good this morning. An you know what I like to do when I'm feeling this way? I likes to pass it on. Can I get a Amen?"

"I'm gone talk a little bit today from the Old Testament. I love the story of Esther because it speaks of a brave woman who risked death and exile to save her people.

"Why I got to talk about that, you say? What's that got to do with anything? Well it's a story that colored folks need to learn from. I see it happening every day ladies and gentlemen.

"Colored folks is the worse people on earth about sticking up for each other. Sadly, a lot of us will sell the souls of our own brothers and sisters if we think we can get somethin' out of it.

"Listen to me now! Stay wit me now. Amen! Ya'll might not like what I'm saying today. But Reverend Scott don' tell no lies. I tell it like it is.

"Now in the book of Esther it tells us that Esther became a queen because of her great beauty. It wasn't because of nothin' else. The woman was beautiful and the king just had to have her," he said, with a little chuckle.

"Anyhow Esther was Jewish. But she decided that she wasn't gone tell the king. One day guided blindly by one of his trusted advisers, the king set out to kill all the Jews in the land.

"Of course this worried Esther. "Cause like I told you, she was Jewish herself. Thank about that now, if you was in her shoes.

"Actually there's several thangs you could do. You could pretend you ain't no Jew, and close yo' eyes to all the killing. You could tell the king the truth and beg for your own life. Or you could do like Queen Esther did and no matter what the consequence, stand by your people.

"Ladies and Gentlemen, this woman was a beautiful queen. She had it all. She didn't want for nothing. But that's not what I want you to remember most about her. I want you to remember that she was willing to give it all away to save her people." He could not hear the Amen's, but the pulse of the church kept him going.

"She was not out to save her own neck. So she asked the king, her king, to spare the lives of all of the Jews in his kingdom."

"How many of you love your people like that? How many of you would be willing to give up all you got to make thangs better for your people."

"Colored folks been working against each other, stabbing each other in the back, since the days of slavery. You ever hear about folks living in the masta's 'big house' thankin' they was better than the colored folks workin' in the fields.

"That kind of stuff still going on now. We ain't slaves no more. But some of us folks thank we better

A. Jean Jackson

than others 'cause we lighter, or 'cause of where we live, or 'cause we got a little money."

Ma Letty shouted, "Amen, Preach, Preach!"

"Ya'll know I ain't lyin'. You better give me a Amen, here today! Is it you?" he said pointing into the congregation. "Are you guilty of turning your back on your own people?"

"We got to do better, ladies and gentlemen. Colored folks have got to do better. We already downtrodden by others in this great land. Why can't we do better by ourselves? Why can't we be more like the beautiful, brave Queen Esther."

Mae Mae listened intently as her eyes never left the Reverend's face. She was spellbound as if his words were meant for her and only her.

When the service was over, the congregation filed from the church. As Mae Mae passed Reverend Scott, she reached out to shake his hand. His large warm hands reached for hers so graciously that she felt like she had known him forever. He was big, but his handshake was gentle and soft.

"And who is this lovely lady, Mizz Letty?"

"This here is Mae Mae," Ma Letty replied. "She like my adopted chile. She been livin' with me for a short spell. An I finally talked her into comin' to church this mornin'."

"Pleased to make your acquaintance, Mae Mae," he said. I hope you enjoyed the service."

"Yeah! Yeah, I sho' did. I liked that story about that queen."

"Oh! I'm real glad you liked it. I hope to see you

here again real soon. When you expectin' that baby?"

"I ain't rightly sho'. But I know it ain't gone be much longer. If I get any bigger, my stomach gone be hangin' down to the ground." She said behind a chuckle.

"Well you take care of that baby when it do get here. I wish you well," he said, as he turned his attention to the person behind them.

In her dream that night Mae Mae saw Jacob. He stood tall and dark, looking down at her in bed. He was dressed in colorful feathers and and beautiful Indian headdress. His smile was just as it had been the last time they made love. It warmed her entire body.

There was a peacefulness in the room soothing her, caressing her. It calmed and relaxed her the same as when they were in 'paradise'.

Mae Mae looked upward and met Jacob's eyes. At that moment, the baby moved inside of her more powerfully than every before. She grabbed her stomach and rubbed gently wanting to comfort the child that suddenly meant everything to her.

Jacob's eyes soothed her as the pains shot through her stomach. She tried to focus on Jacob but her thoughts shifted to Cora Lee.

The screams blasted into the air around her. The dream became reality. Moments later, Mae Mae could hear the sounds of Ma Letty struggling up the steps.

"Can you get to the door to let me in baby," Ma

A. Jean Jackson

Letty shouted from outside the door. "Try to let me in so I can help you."

A sharp pain hit the bottom of her stomach just as Mae Mae reached the door. The door opened as Ma Letty hurried in and helped her back to bed.

"I'm here baby," she said, soothing Mae Mae's head with a wet rag. "Everything gone be alright."

The pains grew stronger as Ma Letty watched the cervix stretch wider and wider, forming a crown around the baby's head. Mae Mae screamed loudly with each new contraction, praying for it all to end.

Finally, with the loudest scream of the night, blood gushed from her bottom, bringing with it the baby they all awaited. Ma Letty placed the bloody baby close to the warmth of the new mother's breast. Crying loudly, the baby signaled her own arrival into the world.

"She beautiful," said Ma Letty, she was still overwhelmed by the phenomenon that had just takin place before her eyes. "I don't think I ever seen a baby that beautiful."

"An I know she Jacob's. I jus' know," Mae Mae announced with delight. "Jacob came to me in a dream. Hold her up so I can see her, Ma Letty."

Ma Letty delivered the afterbirth and tied and cut the cord. She took the baby to the porcelain basin, held her in one hand and washed her tiny body.

"Now you look presentable," she said, handing her to Mae Mae. "See what a handsome girl you got?"

Though tired from her ordeal, Mae Mae was filled with joy at the moment she looked at her baby.

She couldn't get over the eyes. The eyes were the same ones she had seen in her dream before the pains began. They were Jacob's eyes.

"My God! Thank you!" she said. "Thank you for a fine healthy baby. Look at that straight dark black hair, Ma Letty. Look at them cheek bones, an that beautiful copper red skin. She ain't nobody's but Jacob's. Look like he spit her out."

"I'm really happy about that part Chile. I'd sho' hate to see yo' face if thangs didn't turn out like this. What you gone name her? You thought about that?'

"Yeah," Mae Mae said proudly. "Her name gone be Esther, like the queen in the Bible. She gone be beautiful an brave jus' like that."

"That sound real nice *baby*. Now you try to get some sleep. An I'm gone limp back down these steps an try to do the same. Holler if you need somethin', you hear?"

When Ma Letty left, Mae Mae drifted off to sleep with her baby in her arms. This time when Jacob appeared in her dream, he was smiling proudly and waving goodbye.

Chapter 7

As she rocked back and forth, feeling the heartbeat of Esther in harmony with her own, Mae Mae took in the beauty of the snow on the outside. The sound of wood crackling loudly in Ma Letty's pot bellied stove added to the cozy hominess in the room.

Ma Letty's living room was always warm and inviting. The delightful aromas were always drifting from the kitchen, and the happy sounds of Ma Letty's laughter, made Mae Mae and everyone who entered feel right at home.

Curious little objects were everywhere, sitting about on tables like in a museum. Fragile tiny whatnots and little china tea sets filled the tables and shelves. Large cushioned couches and deep comfortable chairs graced the large living room.

Miss Letty's living room was a gathering place. It was everybody's place to relax, or to gossip, or to buy a shot glass of corn liquor. It was the warm loving room where Mae Mae felt closer to Esther than anywhere else in the house.

Love floated freely in the room. All of the love that Mae Mae had in her heart showed in her eyes as she looked at Esther. She felt the smooth silkiness of Esther's soft dark hair while she read out loud. And to Mae Mae the world seemed perfect as the child's tiny fingers grabbed for the faded, yellowing pages of the book in her hand.

Ma Letty listened with pride as Mae Mae carefully sounded out the words in her book. The fingers of her right hand followed the words in each line, touching, feeling, sensing the correct sound before she said it out loud. As she turned the page, large bold letters jumped out from the right top of the page. They read, 'UNCLE TOM'S CABIN'.

'...Well, it is dreadful,' said Eliza; 'but, after all, he is your master, you know.'

'My master! And who made him my master? That's what I think-what right has he to me? I'm a man as much as he is...'

Mae Mae stopped reading, and looked up thoughtfully at Ma Letty. Not only was she reading words, she was understanding them too. Both women, sat in silence for a long moment, not speaking, one not looking at the other.

"Some parts of that book make me so mad," Ma Letty said. "But we need to read it. We got to know the hearts an souls of our people back in those times. It ain't been that long ago. An in some ways Chile, colored folks ain't no better off today."

"Yes mam, I know that," Mae Mae said, closing the book and bringing Esther closer to her chest. "But seem like to me, I ain't been treated much better by my own people.

"You know what I'm sayin', Ma Letty? My own mama sol' me for a hog. A hog! That ain't no better than slave tradin' times. No mam! I can't say colored folks been no better to me."

"Yeah honey, I know you been treated awful in yo' life. But I hope you know, you an Esther is among folks that love you. We care about you. Ain't nothin' bad gone happen to you here."

"I know Ma. Thank you for sayin' that. It feel more like home here with you than I ever felt in my life. I ain't never gone forget all you done for me."

"Now that we done said that an both of us gone be cryin' in a minute, I guess I better take this baby on up the stairs to bed. I got to get up early in the mornin'. I'm goin' to Mizz Logan's tomorrow.

"Night Ma, see you in the mornin'," Mae Mae said, kissing her on the cheek.

The warmth from Esther's little body brought Mae Mae unbelievable joy as she slept beside her. Esther was a small part of Jacob that she could still hold on to and love. She was all that was left of him.

Sleep came quickly for Esther and Mae Mae. Much too soon, the new light of morning was sneaking through the shade. Sleepily Mae Mae eased from the bed. But for a moment she paused. She stopped at the side of the bed and marveled at the beauty of her sleeping daughter.

The rays of the rising sun hit Esther's face and surrounded her head on the pillow like a halo. She hated to disturb her, as she always was forced to awaken her and take her to Ma Letty. But the sun, the face, was a memory Mae Mae took with her as she trudged through the cold snowy streets of Eastend to get to Miss Logan's.

As she walked, Mae Mae looked up at the sky. Though the air was cold and the clear blue sky gave the appearance of warmth. The wind and the snow still were constant reminders of just how cold it was.

The wind wrestled with her. It teased her. It played with the hem of her coat. She held on tightly. She pushed against it, determined to move forward, determined to hold on to the book she clutched under her arm.

When she reached the back door of Miss Logan's house, Viola rushed to let her in. "What in da worl' you doin' walkin' here in dis col' Chile," she said. "I thank you'd walk right through hell ta git ta yo' lessons. Wait a minute. I'm gone tell Mizz Logan you here."

Viola disappeared leaving Mae Mae standing, warming her rear end at the kitchen stove. It was almost painful being so close to heat after a long walk in the cold. But she stooped and turned and rubbed all the parts of her body, praying desperately for the feeling to return.

"Wipe yo' feet good 'fore you go in there on them rugs, lil' gal," Viola said, when she returned. "An be careful. Mizz Sneed in there. She sho' on the war path this mornin'. Come on, Mizz Logan be down in a minute,"

Mae Mae drifted cautiously into the study. Deep inside she spotted Miss Sneed seated on a well padded, bright red Victorian couch.

"Girl! Stop standing there with your mouth open," Miss Sneed growled at Mae Mae.

'Um. Yes mam. I'm waitin' here for yo' sister. Remember, I'm the one Mizz Logan teachin'.'"

"Yes! I'm well aware of that. And what have

you learned, if anything?"

"Well mam, I um. I."

"Just as I thought. All of this time, and you have no idea what you've learned. I told Elynor that teaching Coloreds is a waist of her time."

"No mam!" Mae Mae interrupted with a voice so strong that it surprised them both. "I can read! This book *Uncle Tom's Cabin* is my very own book. An Mizz Logan learned me how to read."

"Mizz Sneed, I don't mean no disrespect. I don't know no big words or nothin'. But I sho' am proud of what I done learned."

"You say you can read. Then read one sentence from that book of yours. Just one sentence."

Mae Mae turned to a page in the middle of the book. It was a passage she knew well. It was marked with a strip of paper. She paused and gathered her thoughts. She was determined to leave a deep, lasting impression. She read slowly, clearly...

'I think you slaveholders have an awful responsibility upon you,' said Miss Ophelia. 'I wouldn't have it, for a thousand worlds. You ought to educate your slaves, and treat them like reasonable creatures, - like immortal creatures, that you've got to stand before the bar of God with.'

"Well, I see you can read," said Miss Sneed. "Now, go over to the coffee table and pour me a cup of tea."

Mae Mae closed her book with an air of pride. Her movement towards the glimmering silver tea service was graceful and confident. She reached for it while keeping her head held high. The steam from the tea rose warming her face as she poured.

"Mizz Sneed," Mae Mae said, as she handed her the cup. "You gone be needin' me to get you anything else?"

"No that'll be all," said Miss Logan, as she entered the room. "Now if you don't mind Jenny, Mae Mae and I have lessons to do,"

Miss Sneed reluctantly rose from the couch. She glanced back quickly at Mae Mae and exited the room.

"I'm very sorry about what my sister just did to you, Mae Mae," said Miss Logan. "That should never have happened to you. In her old age Jenny seems to be angry with the whole world. But surely you can see how different I am from my sister."

"Yes mam. You ain't never been nothin' but good to me. You a true Christian, Mizz Logan. I know my color don't matter none to you. Whatever happened with Mizz Sneed jus' makes me love you more."

They sat together side-by-side listening but not hearing the steady dripping of the melting snow. The sun captured the light of their very different faces. It highlighted the friendship that had formed between them.

Mae Mae called out her words with a loud confidence as Miss Logan listened patiently. With her eyes closed, Miss Logan waited for each word to flow into the air. And without delay, without fail, her student delivered them with perfection.

A. Jean Jackson

"Mae Mae, that was beautiful," said Miss Logan. "I'm so very proud of you. You are reading very well."

"Thank you, Mizz Logan," Mae Mae replied. "You a good teacher too."

When the lesson was over, the two women walked together to the door of the sitting room. Mae Mae moved with her slender grace as she held on to the arm of her matronly companion.

A smile grew on Mae Mae's face as she passed Viola and headed for the door. She was still smiling as she left the house and followed the road towards Padgitt's store.

The stop at Padgitt's became a break from the miserable cold on the walk home. Mae Mae entered with a new air of confidence. Padgitt watched saying nothing as he warmed himself at the red-hot wood stove that sat in the middle of the floor.

Padgitt's wandering eyes escorted her to the counter as Mae Mae stood there and waited. Slowly, at his own pace, Padgitt ventured over to take her money. "That's gone by thirty five cent," he said, spitting a stream of brown juice into a can. "You can't count that out can you?"

"Yessir! Yeah, I sho' can," she said, handing him the correct change.

Padgitt looked back and forth from her hand to his, not believing his eyes. He took the money from her as Mae Mae smiled and skipped playfully out the back door of the store.

Outside she leaned against the wall in the

alley. "Thank you Lord!" she whispered, looking up to the sky.

The hymn she sang as she pushed against the wind towards the end of the alley was a joyful song. It seemed that everything was right with the world. For the first time in her life, Mae Mae was feeling like she was somebody.

But suddenly, as she reached the end of the alley, she stopped her song with the words hanging in the air. She blinked. She blinked again, as if to make the ghost disappear. But to her horror, it would not go away.

"Thought I wasn't gone find yo' ass didn't you," Red said, with yellow teeth flashing through a broad grin.

"How, how you find me?" she asked, shaking from fear as well as from the cold.

"Don't matter. I paid yo' mammy real good for you. I wasn't 'bout to let you get away that easy. It jus' took me a little while that's all. You mine gal. An I'm here to take you back."

"Please! Please, Mr. Red! Jus' leave me be! Please. I been workin'. I got a little bit of money. I'll give it all to you. Jus' leave me be. Please!..."

Mae Mae's heart pounded rapidly as Looney looked on silently. The pounding increased with the fast heavy rhythm of the music from the jukebox.

Looney stuffed his mouth with the last of his chitterlings and rose to leave the cafe. They walked together to the double doors as they dodged late night couples all around them.

    "You see Looney," she said, before he walked out into the darkness of Eastend. "You jus' thought you delivered me from hell when you first brought me here to Ma Letty. But only God knowed, my life of hell wasn't no where near from being over."

Chapter 8

Her tall naked body sunk into the water of the small tin tub as deeply as it could go. She was hoping to disappear and to never to have to return to reality.

The dark smooth nakedness of her body was highlighted by the wetness of her skin. Through the window the moonlight shone on her beautiful wide shoulders, and her narrow, muscular back and waist.

As she washed the smooth hairs between her legs, she could feel Red's eyes burning into her. Through the corner of her eye she spotted him. He was peeping into the window watching her, wanting her.

"Ain't no need in puttin' on them clothes," Red shouted, as he entered the house. "Go on git in that bed!"

With streaks of wetness still on her back, she walked towards the bed. It was the last place on earth she wanted to be. But it seemed to be her destiny. It seemed to be her plight.

He shoved her onto the bed and took hold of her long braided hair. She closed her eyes and prayed. Yet she knew, not even prayer could save her from Red's hell.

Red's penis throbbed in her hand as she massaged it. She knew it well. She knew its powers, she knew its limits. She was determined to keep him from entering her until she was ready. Her plan was to control him in order not to be controlled.

The sounds of Red's moans and the heat of his

breath engulfed her. She shifted her weight under him, trying to avoid his smell. When it became more than she could bear, she closed her eyes and pretended not to be there.

All she could think about was how badly she wanted it to end. And when she heard the onset of his orgasm, she secretly rejoiced. She had commanded it. Just as always, it was the battle she won.

Before he dropped off to sleep, Red rose above her and looked into her eyes. "You ever thank about leavin' here again," he said. "I'm gone kill you. You hear? I'm gone kill you jus' like I killed dat Injun' o' yours. I can do it without even blinkin' a eye."

Once Red was asleep Mae Mae rose and walked to the window. She looked back towards the bed sickened at the thought of being with him again. She hated having to give her body to him.

Her heart beat inside her chest, but only because it was the will of God. It was his plan, not hers. And if it was God's plan for her to be back in hell with Red, she had no reason to want to live.

The moon was smiling at her like a painted picture in the far off sky. Once again it tried to convey hope in a hopeless situation. But this time even the smallest tinge of hope was impossible for her to see.

The next morning as she added a log to the flames of the fire, her utter personal defeat reflected in her eyes. All she could see were the powerful flames jumping, playing inside the fireplace.

The smell of burning pine dominated the air. It popped and crackled being consumed by the powers of the flames. It expelled a warmth she could not feel. It tried to comfort her. But it could touch only the outer layers of her being.

Cold chills ascended her body. She grabbed hold of her shoulders. But it was all in vain. Nothing and no one would ever be able to take away the cold and the pain. Now, the cold dampness lingering in the room was her enemy just like everything else around her.

She leaned way back, resting her head on the back of the chair in front of the fireplace, still staring at the flames. All of her senses gathered together fighting to keep her emotions alive, fighting for a reason to be.

And suddenly it was there. Inside the popping, sizzling flames she saw a small child's face. Big, bright eyes that looked so much like Jacobs, stared back at her through the flames. The face she saw was Esther's. Deep inside the flames, from a place that touched her very soul, Mae Mae saw her reason for living.

Emotions floated around inside her chest. Fear, defeat, guilt, hatred, sorrow pounded on the core of her insides, wanting to get out, wanting to be released. And slowly bit-by-bit, drop-by-drop, it trickled out in her tears.

With a white cloth pressed to her nose, she blew long and deep, clearing her head, preparing for the assault of another day. For a brief moment she turned back towards the flames with a hopeful look. But this time the face of Esther was gone. She patted

A. Jean Jackson

at the moisture under her nose and she began her cooking.

The smell of ham and eggs rose into the air filling the kitchen. The crackling sound of ham frying in the big, black cast iron skillet, made the smell come alive. The sound ended abruptly when she took it out of the pan. The aroma drifted into her nostrils, as she sat the plate before Red, and walked away.

"You sho' this ham done, Gal'?" he said, digging into the eggs. "I don't wont no damn raw meat."

"Yessir, they done," she said not really speaking to him, but knowing she needed to answer.

"When you finish, go on an git dressed," he said. "You going wit' me so I can keep a eye on you."

Later that morning he led her through the woods heading west away from the house. They walked through the graveyard and out into a grassy glade. It was a familiar path to Mae Mae. It was the path through the graveyard that once led her to freedom.

At the end of a long dirt road, sitting inside a halo of the rising sun, the 'big house' stood before her. It was an illusion. Yards from the house, the sparkling beauty and richness of the house teased her. Then steps away, her illusion was shattered.

The white, peeling paint that greeted her was the first sign of just how bad things would be on the inside of the house. The four rickety steps leading to a long porch with lose and rotten planks, led to a door that barely stood on its hinges. But in spite of the poor condition, it was not the door by which they could enter.

They wound around to the rear of the house, walking on a well worn path to the back door. Red knocked and waited, shifting his weight nervously from side to side. With an air of reverence, he removed his hat.

"Mornin' Mizz Harris," he said, looking down.

"This the girl?" she asked, not returning his greeting.

"Yes mam. This here Mae Mae. She a good worker, mam. She'll sho' be happy to do whatever you says. Ain't that right Mae Mae?"

"Yes mam," Mae Mae said, letting Red do most of the talking. "I don't mind no hard work."

"Come on in then," the woman said, gesturing with her hand for Mae Mae to enter the house.

"Ah, Mizz Harris," Red said nervously. "Can I speak to you for jus' another minute."

"What's the matter now, Red?" she said. "The day'll be gone an I ain't gone have no time to work this girl. Now, what the hell you want?"

"Well mam," he said, in a low whispered tone. "Mr. Harris was talkin' about some pay for Mae Mae's work. It ain't gone have to be much," he said, behind a chuckle. "She needin' somethin' to do anyhow.

"She kind of slow in the mind though. An she don't know nothin' about no money. I sho' would 'preciate ya'll jus' handin' that pay over to me."

"Yeah, yeah," said Miss Harris, somewhat irritated. "I don't give a damn who git the pay, as long

A. Jean Jackson

as she work hard an do like I tell her."

"Thank you mam," Red said, tipping his hat.

The pale white woman with a small build led Mae Mae through a junky-screened back porch, into the interior of the house. The woman's long smileless face, with sad blue eyes peeked through stringy, dirty blond hair. Mae Mae stared at the back of her, as she trailed her into the kitchen. Her thoughts turned to Miss Logan.

"They both white," she thought to herself. "But this house and these white folks ain't nothin' like Mizz Logan. Seem like once this used to be a fine house. But they done let it go down. Look like to me they jus' pretendin' to be high class."

The inside of the house was large. But it reeked of a damp musty smell that seemed to feed the ivory vines that chocked the dingy pillars outside. Worn, faded red carpet escorted Mae Mae up the creaky staircase and into each of the rooms.

"This where you need to start," Miss Harris said, pointing into a large bedroom. "Clean an sweep out all these rooms. Dust, make up the beds. After that come down stairs an start on the kitchen. Git yo' cleanin' rags an things out of this closet in the hall."

The muffled steps of Miss Harris tapping on the carpet as she departed drew Mae Mae's attention. Once all was silent, Mae Mae went about her work not feeling, not seeing, not really being there.

After a while, a loud noise outside of the window drew Mae Mae's attention. She pretended to wipe the window sill as she peeped from behind the thick dusty curtain.

The view of Red chopping wood in the cold haunted her as she peered down at him from the upstairs window. In the distance he looked different. He looked smaller. He even looked insignificant from the view she had from the window.

The tears in Mae Mae's eyes threatened to fall as she watched Red shivering in the cold. She felt sorry for him as he wiped his nose with the back of his hand, like a child refusing to come in from the cold.

"You gone watch out that window all day long, or you gone work some today," Miss Harris said, as she came into the room. "You too slow. You should've been down those stairs by now."

"Sorry Mizz," said Mae Mae. "I been workin' real hard 'til jus' a minute ago. Then I seen Red out the window, an I started watchin' a little bit."

"It's always the same," Miss Harris said. "Every time I get a Colored workin' around here they end up bein' lazy as hell. I expect you to work the whole time you here, girl. I don't give a damn who you sees out the window."

"Yes mam. I'm finishin' right now."

Before she left the room, Mae Mae turned back towards the window to close the curtains. As she was closing them, she caught the eye of Red staring up at her. Their eyes met. And she looked him square in the eye for the first time in her life.

That evening as they walked home in silence, they were both tired. And regardless of how cruel her life was. On this day Mae Mae sought the familiarity of

A. Jean Jackson

Red's world. In his world she knew what to expect. She knew what was expected of her.

Just moments away from the shack where they lived, Red regained his power with a shove to her back. As she stumbled through the graveyard, Mae Mae felt more comfortable than she had felt all day long.

She looked over at Red snoozing in and out of sleep after eating a big dinner of fried pork chops, sweet potatoes and collard greens. Light brown haunting eyes opened and closed as if on guard. As usual she waited. But this time she was contemplating how she could tell him the news that he needed to know.

Nothing at all had changed since her return. The dreadful loneliness, the beatings, the brutal sex was still here. But it was the beginning of spring. And the spring of the year always brought change.

"Mr. Red, I think I might be pregnant," Mae Mae said, looking down at the floor. "I ain't had my monthly in a while. An I been kind of sick in the mornins'."

"Well, what in the hell you want me to do," he said. "You still gone go to work at Mizz Harris' house everyday. I don't care how big yo' ass get. You better do what you 'spose to."

For the nine months that Mae Mae was forced to carry the child she knew to be Red's, she hated her body. She hated herself. She hated the fact that she had to question whether she would be able to love her own flesh and blood.

It was a time when she prayed to be beaten. She prayed to be somehow released from the constant reminders of the life growing inside of her.

The morning sickness, the stretching, the pulling, the smells and gaggin, the monster taking over her body made her numb. It made her want to forget the ultimate misery plaguing her soul.

Near the end of her pregnancy, she wished she would explode and have it all over. The moon peeped through the trees, like a giant eye watching over the world. Then suddenly out of nowhere a storm drifted over them.

Lightening darted across the darkness of the sky creating a strange light. And the rains poured like it wanted to wash away all the evil on the earth.

A sharp strike of lightening came towards the window, as Mae Mae ducked behind a chair. Thunder followed the lightning with a loud yet calming thud. And with a brief moment of calm, her water broke sending her liquids onto the floor.

Soon after, when the pains began she thought of Red. With each pain, her hate for him filled the room. With each small emergence of her baby's head, she hated him more. For the moment she remembered Cora Lee. She remembered the hatred Cora Lee had expressed each and every time she gave birth. She remembered Cora Lee cursing the souls of her children. And somehow she understood.

When the baby pushed its way into the world, the unmistakable reddish, nappy hair and the bright brown haunting eyes appeared. And all she could do was try to erase the horrible thoughts that were floating around in her brain.

She held her son close to her chest and cried loud tears. She had to force herself to look at the boy she called Elijah.

Chapter 9

Large oaks looked down on her in judgment as she wandered off into the woods away from the house. Dark, damp moss carpeted her steps. It formed a natural path for her to follow, yet served as her reminder not to venture too far away.

The ground squashed under her feet from the constant wetness. Drops of morning dew lingering on the branches glistened like diamonds, then disappeared drop by drop from the heat of the morning sunlight. The beauty of the morning teased her as she searched for a place in the woods that most revealed the bright blue sky.

Light brown eyes looked up at her smiling, searching her face. But the love Elijah looked for was not there. It had never been there.

The warmth of his little hand burned inside of hers, as she led him to a tree stump in the center of the woods. "Here," said Mae Mae. "Sit right here. An don't you move. You always runnin off, tryin' to see everything. Today, jus' sit yo' little ass down. You hear me!"

Once she seated herself, Mae Mae closed her eyes and welcomed the few moments of solitude she always found in the woods. Her time in the woods was used for reflection. It was her opportunity to try to rediscover the meaning of her existence. It was the time she used to read her book, her only possession that came with her from Ma Letty's. UNCLE TOM'S CABIN was her only link to Ma Letty and Esther. And she had read it so many times that she knew most of it by heart.

Deep in the woods away from Red, she felt safe and at peace. But as she looked up from the pages of her book and glanced over at Elijah, she knew that no matter where she went, hell was always with her.

"Put that damn thing down!" Mae Mae shouted, knocking a colorful mushroom out of Elijah's hand. "I sho' hope you didn't put none of that nasty thing in yo' mouth boy. I swear, with yo' ass I can't turn my back for one minute. You been trouble since the day you was born."

She lifted him off of the ground by one arm and forced his mouth open with her fingers. "Oh my God!" she screamed as she pulled out a small piece of mushroom and smelled his breath.

With his small body dangling in her arms, she rushed him home. As she ran, she prayed. She prayed that she would be able to care if he was dying.

"Why that boy can't hold nothin' on his stomach," Red said, as he entered the house that night. "He usually be eatin' enough for me an you both. Now he throwin' up all over the place."

"I don't know, Mr. Red." Mae Mae said, lying, looking down at the floor. "Must be somethin' he ate. I'm gone keep a real close eye on him. I'm prayin' he gone be alright."

Sleep finally captured Elijah, after hours of convulsive gagging. Peace settled behind his closed eyes as Mae Mae rubbed his wooly red hair.

Black-Eyed Peas and Cornbread

"You know where your name come from, Elijah?" she whispered, with her tears reflecting in the moonlight. "Elijah was a great prophet from the Bible. He always knowed what God wanted him to do. An he swore he wasn't gone never stray from tryin' to please God.

"Elijah, I know I ain't been no Mama to you like I should. But Lord knows! I pray you get well from this. I ain't never wanted nothin' to hurt you."

Sleep swept her away as she sat at his bedside. When she awakened during the night, Elijah wasn't moving. Mae Mae stared for a moment, then quietly placed her hand on his shoulder and shook him.

"Elijah!" she whispered. "Elijah, you alright."

He didn't stir. She shook him again. "I said, Elijah!" she repeated loudly. "Wake up now! Wake up boy! You can't be dead. You jus' can't be."

Her hand gently stroked his face. Warm tears flowed down her face, as she prayed as much for herself as for Elijah.

"God! I know I ain't done right by this boy. It ain't been fair how I treated him, Lord. I know that in my heart. I want the chance to do better. I pray you give me the strength."

Elijah's eyes jerked open as he bent over the side of the bed and vomited a light green slim. Mae Mae held his head and lightly rubbed his back. When he was finished, as he laid his head way back on his pillow, his eyes connected with the eyes of his mother. The caring in her eyes, the gentleness of her touch confused him.

"Thank you Lord!" Mae Mae said, looking up to the sky. "You feelin' any better Baby?" she asked Elijah, with a smile of compassion. "Jus' rest son. Yo' stomach gone feel better tomorrow."

Puzzled by the sudden show of affection, Elijah closed his eyes and savored the moment. Sleep came easily, as he relaxed and enjoyed the softness of his mother's touch for the first time ever.

In the weeks that followed, Mae Mae struggled to open her heart and let Elijah in. She made a conscious effort to look beyond his haunting bright brown eyes. Many times her success at being a good mother to Elijah was determined by how she was treated by Red.

As the sun made its final bow and disappeared majestically through the trees, Mae Mae could tell Red was preparing to leave. By the time it was completely dark and the house was quiet, she climbed into bed alone.

She tossed and turned, as sleep refused to come. There was a mysterious sound. It was calling her, enticing her into the woods. When she could no longer resist, she rose from the warmth of her bed and tipped out onto the porch.

"Sa'day night!" she said with a smile. "Don't a Sa'day night go by that Red don't go to that juke joint. I sho' do wish I could see what go on down there."

Elijah slept soundly as she peeped in on him briefly. She tucked in the sheets around him then ventured back towards the porch. A sweaty palm reached for the knob that closed the door behind her. Fear and excitement took turns controlling the beating of her heart.

On the porch she paused and looked up at the moon. Its crescent shape smiling a half smile, tempted her, dared her to follow the sound.

"Elijah, gone be alright," she said to herself, smiling back at the moon. "Somethin' jus' jumpin' around in the pit of my stomach sayin' there's good times in that juke joint. I got to see that for myself. I ain't gone stay long. I promise."

She followed the stars to the path leading away from the graveyard. Fear gripped her heart. But the moon kept on smiling and Mae Mae kept on walking.

The path just yards from the main road, invited her in. The music drew her closer and closer. The sound was a strange, sinful mix of church music and music that she had never heard before in her life. It was music that jumped around in her soul. And it drew her closer than she ever intended to go.

A large tree close to the window served as her protector. She stooped behind the tree and took in the sights. They were sights such that she had never seen before.

The inside of the juke joint looked as old and run down as the outside. It was shack that looked like a good wind could send it tumbling to the ground. There were holes in the ceiling, and holes in the walls. But nobody seemed to notice.

The only thing that seemed to be holding up

A. Jean Jackson

the old dilapidated shack was the pure heart and soul of the people inside. To Mae Mae there was something magical about the people. Their smiles, the way they moved, made the juke joint exciting.

Dirty barrels that once held bad whiskey, lay all about the inside walls. An old upright piano was in the center of the room. It was putting out a sound as if all of the keys were still there.

The piano was falling apart. But the old grey haired piano player was determined to play the hell out of it anyway. Nothing mattered in the entire room but the sounds of the music and the laughter.

Red's huge stature filled the room as Mae Mae caught a brief glimpse of him through the window. Before she ducked back behind the tree, she caught him draining a shot glass of whiskey.

"Come on here gal, les' dance," she heard him say to the dark fat woman sitting beside him.

"I ain't dancin' with you, you ole fat ass nigga," the woman said laughing, but still grabbing his hand and getting up.

They drifted to the middle of the floor close to the piano. She smiled, as they looked each other in the eyes. Mae Mae held back her laughter as Red wrapped his arms around the woman's waist and grabbed hold of her wide hips.

There was something very relaxed about the way they acted, the way they moved, and drank and danced. Like the little secret world in middle of the woods was the only place they could go to let their hair down. Like the music ringing in their ears could only be heard by them.

Their smiles showed pure colored folks' good times. It revealed their souls. It showed how the spirits of bad whiskey and good times, in a dark, old, shabby room, made them feel like something special.

The women were there for their own selfish reasons. They rolled and grinded their hips while they danced, for their own satisfaction. In this place, even that was alright. In this place they were all completely free to have a good time.

By the end of the night, when they were danced and liquored out, they dozed in rickety wooden chairs. They sat around the barrels that held onto their last shot of whiskey.

If the men were lucky, they had a woman ready to stop in the woods, before starting home. When Red rose to leave, he was drunk but he was alone.

Mae Mae's heart pounded with fear the moment she saw Red heading for the door. She fled into the woods trying desperately to find her way home in the darkness. By the time she reached the graveyard she had to rest. She stopped and she coughed, intensifying the pain in her burning throat.

"He gone kill me," she said to herself. "This time if he catch me, I'm good as dead," she said, moving on towards the house.

When she reached the steps leading to the front door, she tipped up quietly and reached for the knob. She hesitated then breathed a long deep breath. The door opened slowly, creaking in the silence of the night. And as she stepped inside, Red sat waiting.

""Where yo' ass been girl?" he asked, filling the room with the smell of his whiskey.

"No where, Mr. Red," she answered trying to ignore the rapid beating of her heart. "I was jus' out there tryin' to get some air."

"Come here!" he said. "Get down right here. Get on yo' knees right here in front of me."

Mae Mae did as she was told. When she knelt before him, she felt the first of many blows to her face. Red was oblivious to the blood covering his hands, as he reached up to hit her with his fist again and again.

As her consciousness faded, she remembered him on top of her on the floor. His body, almost as limp as hers, weighted her down. But before he could take her, Red was forced to give in to his drunken exhaustion.

The light touch of a small warm hand pressing against her shoulder awakened her the next morning. Elijah's little face inches from hers, looked down at her on the floor. Distorted images danced before eyes that were almost swollen closed from Red's blows the night before.

When she tried to move, pain came alive from every inch of her body. And the child standing before her, looking so much like the enemy who had inflicted the pain, once again became one of the enemy.

"Get off me boy!" she yelled, with hate in her voice. "Seem like after getting' beat by yo' daddy, I wouldn't have to be bothered with yo' ass. Jus' gone an leave me alone."

Elijah toddled away with a renewed sadness capturing his little face. Whatever trust had been restored in the last few weeks was now gone. It was dissolved by the constant evil in which they all lived.

Sunday was supposed to be a day of rest, but Red got up early and was already gone. Mae Mae was restless. She hurt when she sat still and she hurt when she moved. Whatever she did, she hurt. And the intensity of the pain made her hate for Red and for Elijah grow stronger.

"Let's go," she said, as she picked up Elijah and headed out of the door. "I got to get out of here before I go crazy."

The well-worn path into the woods led them to the place where Mae Mae always stopped. The old tree trunk awaited her, sitting in the center of the woods like an old man, broken but wise.

"Now don't you go getting' into nothin' today," she said, as she sat Elijah down. "I ain't gone be rushin' you home cause of no mushrooms today. It's enough I got to put up with that mean ass daddy of yours. I hate that man! I wish he was dead!

"How can I even say that?" she asked herself under her breath. "Ain't no way that evil man gone die, unless I kill him," she said, chuckling to herself. "Hell, I ain't got that kind of nerve. Plus killin' is a sin.

"But Lord, God I can't take these beatins' no more. My face all swoll up. An these bruises all over my body. I jus' can't take it no more! God! What can I do? How can I get away from this hell on earth?

"Mushrooms!" she said, pulling one from the ground. "No I couldn't do that. I can't kill nobody."

A large patch of mushrooms were staring at her. The many colors; the purples, the yellows, the blues drew her closer. She knelt down beside them.

"Can I do it?" she asked, as she nervously picked another mushroom from the damp soil. "God! I got to do somethin'."

She pressed the mushroom to her nose. The softness, the absence of a smell, made them appear harmless as she turned it over and over in her hand.

The colors blended together as she broke it and examined it inside and out. Just looking at it, sniffing it, caused fear and guilt to surge through her body.

"What you lookin' at me like that for boy?" she shouted at Elijah as he looked at her in judgment. "You don't know nothin'! You hear!"

With Elijah looking at her every move, Mae Mae selected the mushrooms she wanted. She wrapped them in a cloth, and tucked them into the pocket of her apron.

All the way home she followed her heartbeat. Her feet stepped lightly on the moist path, but she didn't command them. Her whole being existed outside of itself. The world surrounding her was like a giant cloud. Nothing was real.

The door creaked open with its usual strain. But Mae Mae didn't hear it. Her momentum drew her to the kitchen.

Black-Eyed Peas and Cornbread

Tears fell and mixed with the deadly mushrooms as she chopped them to a fine powder. The tears poured steadily down her cheeks trying to cleanse her soul of the sin she was about to commit. The tears helped to cloud what her eyes were seeing. They helped to make the act easier to complete.

The ritual of chopping became her solace. With each chop, she hummed a song from deep down inside her soul. *'I'm Going Home. My father's house is built on high. Far. Far above the starry sky. I'm goin' home, I'm goin' home, I'm goin' home to die no more.'*

Blackeyed peas, plump from soaking the whole day, were set to boil in a big white pot on the stove. When she stirred in the fat back, ham hocks, and peppers, it filled the room with a thick meaty smell that she knew Red could never resist.

When the aroma was just right, Mae Mae held her breath and poured in the deadly powder. "This gone save my life," she said. "It's gone save my life. But it's gone take my soul."

She wiped her nose with her apron, as if wiping away her uncertainty and fear. Moments later, as Red crossed the yard to enter the house; she poured the last of the deadly powder into a mixture of freshly ground corn meal, buttermilk, flour and baking soda.

"I see you got blackeyed peas an cornbread tonight," Red said, coming in, sniffing the air. "I'm plenty hungry too. When it gone be ready?"

"Ain't gone be much longer, Mr. Red," she said. "Ain't gone be much longer at all."

Her hands shook nervously as she placed a

A. Jean Jackson

platter of hot cornbread in front of Red. He reached for the largest piece, cut it horizontally through the middle and added a sliver of butter. Melted butter rolled down his arm as he lifted it to his mouth.

With crumbs falling all about him, he shoveled a spoonful of blackeyed peas into his mouth and he chewed. His bright brown eyes opened and closed, showing his lust for the food.

Mae Mae sensed everything he was doing, though she didn't look in his direction. She busied herself, trying to move, trying to breath as normally as possible.

"The boy ain't gone eat none of this?" Red asked.

Fear struck her heart like a spear, as she nervously searched for an answer. "Um. No," she said. "He was real hungry this evenin', so I done fed him already."

With each bite, each spoonful placed into Red's mouth, her heart beat louder and louder in her ears. "God what have I done?" she said to herself, as Red belched and rose from the table.

As the sun disappeared on the outside of the house, and the moon and stars claimed dominance over the night, Red dozed in and out of a light sleep.

Before he dropped off completely, he called Mae Mae over to his chair. He looked at her, then jerked her arm pulling her so close she could feel his breath on her face. "Gone git in that bed," he said, in his usual tone.

As the night took on an unusual calm, she went

to the bed and she waited. She waited, but Red never came.

Before the moon disappeared and gave way to the morning, she awakened. Her heart pounded rapidly. It pulled on the pit of her stomach when she discovered that she was still alone in the bed.

Slowly, cautiously she walked to the other room. She could see Red's head leaning off the side of the chair. "Mr. Red!" she called. "Mr. Red, you a'right?"

Not knowing what she would find, she stopped a foot from the chair and faced him squarely. Once it was clear that Red was not going to move, she screamed. She had willed his death. But the sight before her eyes was going to haunt her forever.

Red's light brown eyes were open staring at her. His stare was blank but his eyes held in them an air of revenge. They said to her that somehow for this ultimate sin against him, he would never let her live in peace.

She wasted little time getting her few belongings together to leave. Elijah followed her movement as she went about the house tossing things into a bag. He knew something was different about his life on this day. But what he didn't know was that for a brief moment, Mae Mae had contemplated walking out of the door and leaving him alone.

The morning sun was rising over the ridge. When she left this time she scampered through the graveyard. As she fell and slid and struggled to get away, she carried Elijah but she avoided his light

A. Jean Jackson

brown haunting eyes.

Chapter 10

They watched him move with the grace of a dancer. Each step, each hand movement was done for a special purpose. They were done to make the picture clear, and believable. Words and movement were the tools of his trade.

The pulpit was filled with him. Reverend Scott was a big man. His wide, dark nose held glasses right on the end. The few strands of hair he had, emphasized a dark brown forehead, that always dripped with sweat.

The white handkerchief that was always in his hand, constantly reached for the wetness of his brow, but never dried it completely. Wiping was a part of the dance.

The Eastend crowd believed whatever he said. They needed someone to tell them what to believe. And Reverend Scott could stir up feelings with a power that was going to lead them to salvation.

"What day is this?" Reverend Scott shouted, standing high on the pulpit. "I said, what day is this?"

"This is the day that the Lord has made. Let us rejoice and be glad in it," the congregation echoed back.

He raised his hands high as if reaching for heaven, and commanded with just a gesture, that the choir begin. Mae Mae smiled proudly as Esther's strong alto voice sang lead. She sang with the voice of a woman pouring from the soul of a six year old.

"That's a sangin' chile," Reverend Scott

A. Jean Jackson

shouted. "Can I get a Amen on that? She can sang, an she a pretty lil' thang too," he said laughing. "Ya'll know what I mean this mornin'."

The congregation laughed as the Deacons shouted their own special Amen. Mae Mae looked about knowing all eyes were on Esther, her little angel.

Since the day Mae Mae returned to Asheville carrying Elijah in her arms, she noticed that Esther was the perfect child. An now, in church as she sang her heart out, Mae Mae glowed with pride.

"Am I my brother's keeper?" the Reverend shouted, as he stepped back from the podium and wiped sweat with the handkerchief he pulled from his sleeve. "You ever think about the story of Caine and Able? Can you believe a man would kill his own brother?"

"No! No Lord!" he heard a distant voice shout back.

"An you know what he had the nerve to ask," the Reverend questioned, not waiting for an answer. "Am I my brother's keeper?

"But! My God knows all, ladies an gentlemen. I don't know 'bout yo' God," he almost whispered with a chuckle and a skip. "But my God, he knows all. He knew what Caine had done.

"And Caine still asked, 'Am I my brother's keeper?'

"Let me break it down for you a lil' bit right here."

"Yes! Yes, break it on down. Break it down

now," Deacon Johnson chimed in, clapping his hands and stomping his feet.

"You know, God's jus' like yo' mama. Say Amen! He gone always give you a chance to tell him what you done. But! He already know!

"I tol' you. My God know all!

"That's the thang Caine must of forgot. Cause seem like he thought he didn't need God. He thought once he killed Abel things was gone be jus' fine.

"But jus' tryin to tote around that secret was too much to bear. You can't do evil behind yo' mama's back," Reverend Scott said with a chuckle. "An you sho' can't fool the Lord my God. My God, he knows all."

With the wave of his hand, he began a loud, commanding, off key, *"A-A-Men."* The congregation answered with an enthusiastic, *"A-A-Men."* Then, all of the voices, good and bad alike, blended together in a spiritual, hand clapping, display singing, *"A-A-Men, A-Men, A-Men."*

Reverend Scott stepped away from the pulpit and jumped down into the isles. As he jumped up and down and around to the rhythm of the clapping, pure unadulterated soul poured out all over the church.

"In the mor-nin', A-A-Men. This glorious mornin'. A-A Men, A-A-Men, A-Men, A-Men."

With another wave of his hand, the singing ended. "Ya'll sangin' that song like you know somethin', he said. "You know what I mean, don't you. You sangin' it like you know he love you. An he do. He really do.

A. Jean Jackson

"You know, anybody that can love you when you do wrong, that's love. God love you jus' like he loved Caine. All he wants you to do is ask to be forgiven. Jus' ask."

Mae Mae looked at Elijah and she saw Red. The haunting look from Elijah told her that the forgiveness the Reverend spoke of was meant for her and only her.

"Sister Mae Mae," Reverend said with a big smile, as they filed out of the church. "I ain't throwin' no hints or nothin'. But I been hearin' about what a fine cook you is. They say ain't no one in all of Asheville that can beat yo' cookin."

"Well Reverend, I ain't gone say all of that," Mae Mae replied, blushing. "But we'd sho' be glad to have you to supper today. Ma Letty got some chickens, so I'm gone be fryin' a couple. We'd love to have you."

"OK. I'll sho' enough be there this evening."

Just before dusk, the Reverend with his shiny black suit and smiling white teeth appeared. With him, came the dampness of a light evening shower and a rainbow that slowly disappeared with the setting sun.

As he entered the house, excitement filled the air. Having a preacher at the dinner table was the next best thing to God himself.

"Look like you enjoyin' that fried chicken pretty good," said Ma Letty, joking as the Reverend licked his fingers.

"Sho' is mighty good. Sho' is," he said.

Black-Eyed Peas and Cornbread

"Sister Mae Mae," Reverend said, after they all finished and drifted from the table. "I sho' would be pleased to have you walk out with me. The porch air mighty nice after that rain."

"Sho' Reverend," She said, grabbing a sweater.

"I'm so glad I came this evenin'," he said, looking at the stars. I know you probably ain't never thought nothin' about me. But I been lookin' at you. I'd be pleased to keep company with you.

"I know it's real soon to be sayin, but you young an I'm a ole man. I got to git on with my life quick as I can," he said smiling nervously.

Mae Mae looked puzzled. But she remained silent. She waited to see what the Reverend was really trying to say.

"I can give you a good life," he continued. "I can give you an yo' children a good Christian life."

"Ah! Reverend Scott," Mae Mae said. "I ain't never thought about you like that."

"I know but I want you to think about it. I imagine yo' life been hard. Think about yo' children. I can afford to give ya'll the kind of home that you deserve."

That night Mae Mae couldn't sleep. Instead, she stood in the darkness of the room and gazed at her sleeping children.

"They so different," Mae Mae, thought to herself. "These children different as night an day. I don't know. Sometimes I jus' don't know what's best for them.

A. Jean Jackson

Esther with her thumb in her mouth, rolled over seeking the warmth of her blankets. Elijah tossed and turned, sweating, throwing his blankets to the side of the bed.

"God I been back here over a year," she said, still thinking aloud. "Ma Letty, bless her heart. She took me back in with my son, jus' like I ain't never left.

"All that time I was gone, she took care of Esther jus' like she was her own. Now my baby girl six years ole. An Ma Letty sho' done raised her right. I'm mighty proud of that girl.

"Esther been tryin' her best to love Elijah. But that lil' devil, he mean. Poor chile, he jus' ain't got no love in him. I guess a lot of that's my fault. It's jus' hard for me to feel anything for that chile.

"Lord! Tell me what to do! I don't want to marry that ole preacha. But maybe he's what I need. Maybe he's what these children need. I jus' don't know.

"Elijah sho' need some Christian raisin'. He need a father in his life. I ain't never been able to give that boy what he need. Can't say I'm ever gone be able to.

"An Lord, more than anything else. I'm seekin' forgiveness for this deep dark secret I'm carryin'. Maybe marryin' that preacha is jus' what we all need.

Months later, following a brief courtship, St. James Church was buzzing with gossip. The Reverend stood proudly at the alter as Mae Mae joined him to exchange their vows. Though she had faced such a difficult life that she felt old before her time, the yet to be twenty-eight year old bride was especially beautiful beside the much older groom. Preacha was more than fifteen years her senior.

The ceremony was simple. The plain white dress against her dark smooth skin reminded her of the cleansing she sought for her sins. When she stood before all of Eastend joining with Preacha in marriage, she was asking for the ultimate forgiveness.

When all of the excitement was over and she said her goodbyes to Ma Letty, she took her children by the hands and took them home. Preacha opened the door to the house and carried Mae Mae over the threshold with Esther and Elijah trailing behind. He placed her carefully on the soft beige carpet.

Inside the house, everything was in place. The large cushioned chairs in the living room matched the couch that wound around the entire room. The shiney coffee table, centered just right, held the beautiful ceramic vase overflowing with fresh, red, long stem roses.

Each room of the house had it's own personality. And Mae Mae's favorite room, the well equipted, large kitchen, looked like it had been awaiting her for a long, long time. The house, the status of being the minister's wife, the fact that they were now a real family, made her believe she was finally somebody.

The bedroom was much larger than the whole house she had grown up in with Cora Lee. The large bed looked back at her innocently with its perfectly white ruffled spread. She knew well what went on in

A. Jean Jackson

the bed of a man at night. She had learned that lesson way ahead of her time. The difference was that with Preacha, she was a willing partner. For the ultimate forgiveness she sought, being with Preacha was not too much to ask.

"Mama this house is really big," Esther shouted running into Preacha's and Mae Mae's room. "And I've got a room of my own."

"Shut up girl!" Elijah shouted back. "You act like this house is so great."

"It is," Mae Mae interupted. "Niether one of you ain't never had a room of your own or an inside bathroom. So both of you better be damn glad you here."

"Ooh! You can't be cussin' around Preacha's house," Elijah said, giggling.

"OK! OK! I won't cuss. Now, ya'll go on and unpack. We all gone turn in early."

Preacha listened to the exchange and simply smiled. He retired for a while to his study, happy to escape the newness of the lively activity in his house.

On her wedding night, Mae Mae opened and closed her eyes trying her best to shut out memories of Red. She laid beside Preacha and she gave him her body in hopes of giving her children a better life, in hopes of saving her soul.

"Ain't no way I can go wrong this time," she thought, as she let him caress her body. "I can't get no closer to God than this."

Black-Eyed Peas and Cornbread

Times were always happy for Esther when Preacha came home. He walked towards the two children and the distinct melodic whitsle that always accompanied him, got louder. When he reached them, just like always he looked in Esther's direction and smiled. In Elijah's mind, Preacha's smiles were always meant for Esther.

"Hey sunshine," he said.

"Hey," she said, waiting anxiously for what always came next.

"You been good today, Elijah," he said, barely looking his way.

The children stood facing Preacha with Elijah standing directly behind Esther, more for an understood importance than because of height or age. But the game was always the same and the outcome was always worth it for them both.

"Close your eyes," Preacha said, knowing they always complied to his request. "Now reach in my pocket and pull out yo' surprise. You go first, Sunshine."

Esther reached in, like always. Her small hand wandered deeply into Preacha's pocket and felt around for the surprise. With the slow guidance of his hand, she always found it. And the loudness of his laugh was another signal of her success. It showed that he loved her finding it as much as she loved the game.

When she emerged from his pocket, she could already smell the strong scent of peppermint. Closing her eyes, was a part of the game but the prize, the

A. Jean Jackson

feel, the smell of it was always the same, and Esther was never disappointed.

"My turn! My turn," Elijah shouted, knowing the game was really already over.

"OK," Preacha said. "Come on then. Reach in and get your prize."

The candy in the left pocket awaiting Elijah was always right there at the top. He reached in with no real excitement, no smile. He took his candy from the pocket like a hunter, like a man obsessed with having what he thought he deserved. His eyes shown brightly as he placed the candy into his mouth. It was a satisfaction beyond sweetness.

With Preacha gone, Esther teased Elijah, sucking and savoring the candy in her mouth. She knew her piece was always bigger. She knew it was given with more delight. But Elijah was quiet. His candy was long since gone. Bitten, cracked and swallowed, it was gone before Preacha's scent had left their nostrils.

"Where's yours?" she said, teasing, holding a piece outside her mouth for effect.

"Gone," he said, knowing she already knew.

"Want a piece of mine?"

"Yeah!" he said with anticipation that was never fullfilled.

"Well, you shouldn't 've ate yours so fast," she said with a snicker.

"I knew you wasn't gone give me none," he said, more angry about the teasing than not getting the candy. "I hate yo' ass. An I'm gonna get you. You jus' wait."

She walked away knowing that the threat he made was true. He always got her back. And now, it was just a matter of time.

The place in the house where Mae Mae could see the children grow most was at the table. Each meal, each day, each year, their new life, their life with Preacha seemed to emerge at the dining room table.

One moment Elijah was barely visible over the table's edge, and the next moment, he sat tall with his face taking on the features of Red more prominently than ever before. And the more he grew and looked liked his father, the more Mae Mae hated her own son.

Esther's beauty blossomed at the table, day by day, year by year. Her rich caramel colored skin and her flowing dark hair shown brightly, reflecting in the smooth, beautiful mahogany table. Mae Mae looked at her proudly each day, watching the face, the mannerisms of Jacob appear before her eyes.

Preacher looked across the table and the constantly emerging differences of the members of his family had grown more obvious than ever before. This was a predetermined family with no blood ties to him, that had surrounded him for years at the table. And though he had molded them to fit into his environment, he was the true outsider.

Mae Mae, his wife, was not his true love. He had known that from the first time they were together

A. Jean Jackson

in his bed. He knew she could never really be his. He knew that they were each other's convenience. The roles cast him as the well-respected minister, and her as the beautiful minister's wife. And over the years, both of them had learned their roles well.

Preacha loved his family for the most part. But to him, Elijah was just, 'the boy'. Preacha could make nothing else of him. He was not even a likable boy and Preacha refused to take on the manly interest in him that Mae Mae so desired. In fact, he realized that he and Elijah were both outsiders in the scheme of things.

The difference was that Elijah could always be sacrificed by anyone in the family. Preacha on the other hand was what they all needed for their sense of home and family, even if only for appearances sake. This was the ransom that Preacha had held for years.

White sheets flopped in the wind in the fall of 1938 as Mae Mae hung clothes on the line. She hummed softly and glanced over the line at the house she cherished. A perfect large yellow house with white shutters and flower filled window boxes, smiled at her from the distance.

The sound of crunching leaves led her back towards the house. She stopped, turned and looked back down the hill. The sheets glared back at her, selfishly capturing the sunlight, and shining back with a white perfection.

She climbed up the back steps onto a small

high porch and entered through the back door to the house. Freshly starched curtains and a spotless linoleum floor met her at the door.

She glanced at the freshly cut wild flowers sitting on the kitchen table, and the neatly placed dishes drying in the drain. But then, her heart stopped as she discovered Esther sitting, crying on the other side of the room.

"What's wrong baby?" she asked, walking towards her. "You look like you jus' seen a ghost."

"Nothin'," Esther said, as she burst into tears.

"Wait jus' a minute now. You ain't sittin' over there cryin' yo' eyes out for nothin'. What happened? Tell me Chile!"

"Preacha! I'm scared o' Preacha."

"Why? Did he do somethin' to hurt you Chile?"

"Preacha made me get in the bed with him. He said it's a father's job to get their girls ready for marryin'. He said it's between him an me."

"He did what!" Mae Mae shouted, as thoughts of Red surged her brain. "Damn him! God! Why my chile got to go through the same pains I had to. I trusted that man him with my angel."

Esther sobbed louder with each curse word that erupted from Mae Mae's mouth. "Why he do it Mama?" she said. "I was scared. I was scared the whole time."

"I know how you hurtin' baby. I know better than anybody else. That kind of hurt don't never go away. I'll kill him. Nobody ain't gone hurt my baby girl like I been hurt in this life."

A. Jean Jackson

"Mama! Mama! don't say that. Please don't. Don't kill him 'cause of me."

"Jus' let me take care of Preacha, you hear. I jus' want to know you a'right? That's all I want to know right now."

"I guess I'm OK. But my heart hurts, Mama. It hurts real bad."

"I'm so sorry, I can't do nothin' to fix that baby. But I've got to do something. I've got to find Preacha before I go crazy."

The softness of her breasts pressing against his back was the first thing he felt. The muscles in her neck and shoulders flexed with an air of strength and determination. Without even turning around, he could tell that she was ready for battle.

"Ah! What's wrong, honey?" Preacha said nervously.

"You know what you done," Mae Mae said almost in a whisper, close to his ear. "I hear you messed with my Esther."

"She lyin' Mae Mae," he said. "I wouldn't do nothin' like that to that chile."

Sweat poured from Preacha's head just like he was preaching hard on a Sunday morning. He didn't turn around. He was scared to look at her.

"I got a notion to kill yo' ass sittin' right there in that chair," Mae Mae said. "The only thing keepin' you alive is Esther begged me not to kill you. I don't want that chile to have yo' dead ass on her conscience along with the other shit you done shamed her wit'.

Black-Eyed Peas and Cornbread

"If you ain't out of this town before Sunday service, you gone be sorry. I'm gone be like a black cat rubbin' up against you for the rest of yo' life if you ever come around me or my family again. An just remember this...Killin' somebody that done evil to me and those I love, ain't nothin' new for me. I got one on my soul, so two can't matter that much."

On those final words, she walked slowly out of the room. Elijah's shadow darted passed the door. But when she reached the hall he was gone.

"Was you at that door listenin' boy?" she asked, when she saw Elijah in the kitchen. "I saw you."

"Yeah, I was listenin'," he said, looking up with those light brown eyes she hated. I heard you talkin' to Preacha."

"Whatever you heard boy, you better keep it between me an you. You hear me!"

"Yeah! Yeah! I hear you," he said, looking away.

"Now go get yo' things. We goin' back to Ma Letty's."

Chapter 11

Fluffy white pillows surrounded her head like soft floating clouds. The large bed that held her, created the appearance of a queen waiting to be served.

The loud hearty laugh that Mae Mae had missed, filled the room as she and her children entered. Ma Letty's face lit up brighter than the sun peeping through the window over her bed.

As she opened her arms wide enough to hold them all, a happy spirit filled the room. But Mae Mae could tell by the sick eyes and the weak, slow movements, that Ma Letty was not well.

"My babies! My babies done finally come home," said Ma Letty. "I ain't been feelin' all that good. But jus' seein' ya'll jus' done made my day."

"Ma Letty, what's wrong?" said Mae Mae with concern in her voice. "I didn't know you was this sick."

"Yeah darlin'. I been sick just a short spell now. You ain't had no time to keep up with my hard times. But Lordy! Now that my family back, I'm gone be up an around in no time."

"Ma! I'm sorry I ain't been around when you needed me," Mae Mae said, with tears in her eyes. "I'm gone take care of you now. We back. We ain't never gone leave you again."

Ma Letty settled comfortably into her pillows. She could feel the warmth of Mae Mae's hand as she held it and drifted off to sleep. As the daylight began to fade, a single ray of sunlight touched her face.

Black-Eyed Peas and Cornbread

Mae Mae and her two children sat beside her and watched. They watched as their thoughts surrounded Ma Letty's bed. A lot was revealed in the face of the sleeping Ma Letty. These were revelations none of them could see.

Esther looked off into the distance. The usual childlike innocence was absent from her face. At this point she trusted nothing. She didn't even trust the family who sat there beside her.

Elijah's bright brown eyes were magnified even in the darkness. They showed a wisdom far beyond his years. He could see the pain in his mother's face. He could see Esther's broken heart, and Ma Letty's sickness. Elijah could see it all. But he felt nothing.

"What in God's name happened over there Chile," Ma Letty whispered to Mae Mae the next morning. "I didn't want to ask around the children. But I could tell time I saw you, somethin' awful bad was on yo' mind."

"Ma how could I have trusted that man with my beautiful lil' girl?" Mae Mae said, crying. "That man a preacha, Ma! He supposed to be a man of God. And he raped my lil' angel."

"Mae Mae!" Ma Letty shouted. "I'm so sorry, honey. Tell me he didn't do that. Tell me he didn't go messin' with Esther. Why in the worl' he want to mess with that chile?"

"I don't know Ma. But I could of killed Preacha for doin' that. After sufferin' so much jus' like that when I was younger, I could of killed him real easy."

A. Jean Jackson

"Hush Chile! Don't be talkin' like that. You couldn't never kill nobody. That ain't even in you, so don't be even sayin' it."

Mae Mae looked away. She didn't want Ma Letty to see her face. The big sin of her life would be given away by her face. It was a sin she never wanted Ma Letty or anyone else to know about.

"Ma I ain't never really trusted no man. But I guess I thought Preacha was different. I thought nothin' but good could come of him. In my heart, I wanted him to be a Godly man. But I was wrong. I was wrong and it might have cost me my Esther."

"She gone be hurtin' for a long time baby," Ma Letty said, in a low calm voice. "Ain't nothin' you can do about that. Jus' keep on givin' her love. That's about all you can do.

"An give some love to that boy too. Somethin' ain't right with him, chile. There's a real emptiness deep down in them bright brown eyes. Can't nobody love that boy but you."

"I been tryin' Ma. I been tryin' since the day he was born. But it's so hard. I guess I done messed up with both of my children. Seem like evil jus' follow wherever I go. Seem like if I lived with God, I'd still be runnin' from the devil."

Mae Mae stood to leave. The sadness in her voice trailed in the air behind her as she went through the door.

By late afternoon, the sun was at its height as it poured through Ma Letty's window. The warmth coming from it felt good as it caressed Ma Letty's skin. The sky, colored in brilliant blue, served as the perfect backdrop as she settled back in her pillows and prayed.

Hurt and pain shattered Mae Mae's heart as she glanced at Esther trying to hide herself in a dark corner of the kitchen. Mae Mae knew her daughter's pain, she knew her thoughts, her feelings of helplessness. She wished and prayed that as a mother she could take it all away.

Mae Mae walked over and took Esther by the hand. Neither of them spoke. There were no words that could possibly express the love and kinship between them at that moment. The warmth of Esther's hands reminded Mae Mae of the baby who had sat upon her lap years before. But the reality of the moment made it much too clear. Esther was no longer a child.

Mae Mae poured scalding hot water from the kettle into the tin tub sitting in the middle of the floor. The mixture of hot and cold created a rising steam, like ghosts escaping into the air. Esther stepped in, guided by Mae Mae's hand. She sunk deeply, down to her shoulders, wishing to cover herself. Mae Mae's primary objective was to cleanse her daughter's life, to cleanse her existence. By taking the cloth in her hand and sprinkling water slowly over Esther's back, she wanted to soothe her, to take away her misery with the warm water, by her very touch.

Esther's radient beauty shined forth. It was enhanced by the wetness covering her body. But even with such radiant beauty, especially pronounced by the presence of them both sitting there together so intimately, they sensed only the ugliness in the room.

Esther's body smiled, taking in the touch of her mother's love. At that moment and in that time, that was what both of them needed.

In the months that followed, it was apparent to Mae Mae that nothing would ever be the same. Her fairy tale life with Preacha was over. She and her children's lives were forever changed. And Ma Letty was not the same physically strong woman they'd left years before.

Though Elijah was quiet, he was well aware of his suddenly changed environment. He had learned early in life, not to trust anyone and to always look for any weaknesses that surrounded him. Immediately upon their arrival, Ma Letty became his prey.

She could feel him watching her through the opened door. He said nothing. He just walked by and stood moments at a time as she pretended to be asleep.

Finally, she called to him. "Elijah! Elijah! Come here boy. You hear me callin' you boy."

He peeped in, surprised that she had acknowledged him. "Yeah, Ma. What you want?"

"I been seein' you, boy," she said. "You jus' watchin' me like a vulture waitin' to suck my bones. What's yo' problem, boy? What in heavens name is wrong with you?"

Elijah looked around the room. When he was

sure he was the only one around, he moved close to her. "Ole lady! Why don't you go on an die," he said. "I don't care nothin' about you. I want to see you die. I ain't never seen nobody die before."

"You evil!" Ma Letty shouted in a weak voice. "You lucky I ain't got the strength. Cause if I did, I'd sho' enough give you the beatin' you been needin' for a long time.

"I been dreamin' about you boy. I might as well say they was nightmares though. Can't say I know what they mean. But I know one thing. I didn't like what I seen. I didn't like how they made me feel.

"I kept on seein' yo' strange lookin' bright eyes lookin' at me through big flames of fire. An I was reachin' for you. I don't know why. I don't know if I was reachin' tryin' to help you, or if you was reachin' to help me.

"It's strange boy. Something jus' ain't right with you. I jus' hope I live to see the day you find the Lord. Seem like to me you need him in yo' life real bad. Now gone get out of my sight an let me rest."

"Don't worry," Elijah said laughing. "Look like you already got one foot in the grave."

His laughter echoed through the house sending shivers down Ma Letty's spine. The silence that fell afterwards enveloped the house and left behind an impending doom that refused to go away.

Elijah's mean spirit was always around. It was like a dark cloud over his head that everyone could sense. At home, at school, where ever he went he was hated. His life at school, among his peers, simply fueled his terrible homelife.

He looked about the classroom, and though he saw many faces he felt alone. His finger gently caressed the word "Pussy", carved neatly and deeply into the wood. Elijah, with a certain precision that never reflected in his schoolwork, had carved it into his desk early in the year.

His desk mocked the ragged appearance of everything else in the dingy schoolroom. The water stained ceiling, the cracked plaster, and decaying wooden floor were fixtures in his learning environment.

The smell of greasy breakfasts and smoky hair mingled in the air as the school day began. Elijah bowed his head in reverence to the morning prayer. But his thoughts were somewhere else.

"Esther the only one she care about," he said to himself. "Mama don't give a damn about what I do. She ain't never cared nothin' about me. I'm gone fix 'em though. I'm gone fix 'em all."

Chalk squeaking on the old cracked blackboard captured Elijah's attention. A crude drawing of North America was forming before his eyes. He saw the drawing, but his eyes followed Miss Rone's wide hips shaking to the rhythm of her writing.

When she turned to face the class Elijah blinked back his thoughts and drifted in and out to the sound of her monotonous voice. "Which one of you can tell me the continent you live on?" she asked. "Raise your hands if you know the answer. Come on everybody. Raise your hands high."

Elijah looked away avoiding her eyes. His hand was not raised. "I don't know. An I don't care," he thought, smiling in the privacy of his brain.

"OK! Wallace. What's the answer?" she continued.

"North America," Wallace sang out to the class.

"Lil' sisy," Elijah thought, glad Miss Rone didn't call on him. "He think he know so damn smart."

"That's right, Wallace. Very good," said Miss Rone. "And what countries make up the North American continent? Somebody else, anybody. Ya'll suppose to know this. Elijah, do you know?"

"Oh shit!" he said, under his breath. "Why that lady got to call on me. Um! Um! I don't know Mizz Rone," he said.

"Elijah. Did you not study your geography chapter last night?" she asked, with a firm voice.

"No."

"No! What!" she shouted.

"No, Mizz Rone."

"That's right. You show respect when you're talking to adults boy. Do you hear me?"

"Yes mam," Elijah said, looking down.

His head was spinning. He wanted to reach up and grab her by the throat. He wanted to squeeze the life right out of her. It was obvious that she didn't like him.

"Well young man," Miss Rone said. "If you refuse to read your lessons at home, I'm going to make sure you read them here. Now take your books

A. Jean Jackson

and go the corner of the room. By the end of the day, you better know the next two chapters of this geography book. Do you understand?"

"Yes Mizz Rone," he said, walking to the back of the class in the midst of his chuckling classmates. "I hate school," he said to himself. "I hate Mizz Rone and everybody else."

By the end of the day, when Miss Rone rang the bell, Elijah was so full of anger that he ran from the room. He headed for home, not knowing if he really wanted to be there either.

The rocks and dust along Dirty Eagle Street scattered under his feet as he kicked angrily at the ground. The long walk home from Beaufort Street School back to Eastend, along the dirt road gave him time to think.

"What you learn in school today Elijah?" Mae Mae asked, as he came through the door.

"Nothin'," he said, not wanting to talk.

"Well, seem like I'm sendin' you to that school for more than that. I ain't never had the chance to get my learnin' like that. You an Esther is mighty lucky you able to sit up in the schoolhouse with a teacher all day."

"Lucky!" he said, sarcastically.

"You better be behavin' yo'self, I know that," Mae Mae shouted. "An don't be comin' in here sayin' you ain't learned nothin'. You better come in here everyday tellin' me about somethin' you done learned. Now, where Esther, she didn't walk home with you?"

"No. I didn't wait for her. I wanted to walk by

myself."

"OK. Go on an feed Ma Letty's dogs. Then get yo'self cleaned up for dinner. I'm gone feed everybody early tonight. Then I'm goin' to spend some special time with Ma."

Mae Mae was deep in thought as she filled platters of fried fish, stewed corn and cabbage and placed them on the table. The strong fishy smell was still all over the house when they sat down to eat.

Everyone at the table carefully picked out the little bones while they gobbled down the soft white meat and the other food on their plates. They ate in silence, as everyone knew that without Ma Letty, something special was missing. Mae Mae ate, cleaned up then retired from the kitchen.

"Hey Ma. How you feelin'?" Mae Mae said, as she plopped down in a chair beside the bed.

"Lil' gal," said Ma Letty, with a weak voice. "Did I ever tell you how much I love you?"

"Yeah Ma," Mae Mae replied, taking her by the hand. "You show me everyday. You been like a mama to me since the first day I saw you."

"You the chile God gave me, Mae Mae. I couldn't have had a better daughter if I birthed you myself. Now go on to bed. You don't have to sit here with me Chile. I know you tired."

"I'm alright Ma. I'm gone jus' sit here with you a while. I miss bein' around you. I want you to git better."

Mae Mae held Ma Letty's hand as they sat in silence. They dozed together, drifting in and out of sleep as darkness fell on the room. Everything was completely quiet, until both of them were awakened by a noise in the hall. When Me Mae saw that everything was alright, she rose to leave.

"Look like you gainin' some weight Chile," Ma Letty said followed by the laugh that Mae Mae loved. It filled the room as Mae Mae smiled and kissed her goodnight. It echoed throughout the entire house.

Once in her own bed, Mae Mae gave in to the fatigue. She settled in warming the sheets with the movement of her body.

The house, the room was unbelievably quiet until suddenly her mind came alive as she raised up in bed and the unmistakable smell of smoke grabbed her nose.

She rose higher. She wanted to make sure all that was happening was not a dream. When there was no doubt in her mind, she shouted in a loud shattering voice, "fire!" She jumped up, put on her robe and quickly awakened her sleeping children.

On the way down the steps, in the midst of suffocating layers of smoke, she shouted for Ma Letty. She shouted, but she knew there was no way to save her. Beautiful but destructive flames engulfed the house as she ran out and stood with the other survivors. Everyone was there. Everyone except Ma Letty was there looking back at the flames.

Tears poured from Mae Mae's eyes as she screamed while reaching helplessly to the sky. "Ma! Ma! My God, Ma!" The words drifted into the air with the smoke.

Black-Eyed Peas and Cornbread

Esther held onto Mae Mae, touching, comforting. She cried with her, for her, for herself, for Ma Letty. But as Mae Mae caught the light of the flames reflecting in the bright brown eyes of Elijah, he was smiling.

PART II

She sat gazing out of the window, watching the slow steady drizzle of the rain. The lonely sounds of the New York streets seemed to come alive with the short rain shower. But Esther hated the rain. The rain always brought with it a damp dreariness that reminded her too much of home.

Esther lit a cigarette and forced the smoke into the air as she sat on the side of the bed. Lighting up a cigarette, when she was in a thoughtful mood was as natural for Esther as breathing.

The tiredness from late night shows in dark, smokey nightclubs showed in her eyes. But the only time she ever felt good was when she was performing. She needed the praise. She needed the love that came back to her from the audience. Even though the love only lasted as long as the applause, she still needed it.

There was so much hurt, and pain she was trying to forget. She thought she could simply run away, and leave it all in Eastend. She thought it could be buried deep in another terrible family secret. But it was too vivid in her mind. The memories came back to her each and every day...

Chapter 12

"Girl!" Mae Mae said. "I see that look on yo' face. An I ain't likin' what I'm seein'. You still worried about yo' clothes ain't you?"

"Yeah," Esther said. "It ain't like when you was this age Mama, here in 1941, at Stephens Lee High School, everybody goes the first day with somethin' new on. I know we ain't got no money. I jus' hate bein' so different, that's all."

"We doin' the best we can, Chile," Mae Mae said, with sadness in her voice. "I ain't had no pot to piss in since Ma Letty died. An all you can think about is havin' somethin' new on yo' back to go to school.

"You jus' don't know how proud I am of you, Esther," Mae Mae said, changing her tone. "Ain't nothin' in this world make me prouder than you goin' off to Stephens Lee High School. Nothin'."

"But we livin' in these cramped up rooms that ain't even ours. Lord, Reverend Henessey was sweet as he could be lettin' us live here. But I don't know how much longer he gone let us. We could be out in the street before you know it."

"So Chile, wear what you got. It ain't new, but it's clean. An all the while you wearin' it, hold yo' head up high."

Esther's drudgery came more to life as she struggled up the steep hill leading to Stephens Lee. She looked down at the worn heels on her shoes and her faded blue skirt and pink blouse. But as her hand reached for the door handle to go inside, suddenly it

A. Jean Jackson

didn't matter.

Frank Jordan stood waiting on the other side. He smiled his broad beautiful smile as he held the door for her.

"Mama couldn't stand Frank," Esther said to herself, flicking her ashes into an empty soda bottle. "But he respected the hell out of her. He claimed he didn't understand her. But he did respect her."

"I guess it was because of the café. I mean, she was the only Colored woman anybody in Eastend ever saw own her own café. In our world, Colored folks didn't own nothin' at all. I was proud of Mama myself."

"I couldn't believe it when she got all that money. That white man came out of nowhere. An a few days later, she was buyin' the café..."

He climbed the steps approaching the door with caution. Peeping into the screen door he knocked timidly.The unfamiliarity of the neighborhood, the house, and the people watching his every move showed in the redness growing on his face. He smoothed back his blond hair and knocked again. This time the knock was louder.

Mae Mae rose from her chair while curiously looking out. She looked through the screen, saying nothing. She waited for the nervous White man to state his business.

"Good afternoon mam," the man said. "I'm James Whisett of Interstate Global Insurance

Company. Are you Mae Mae Scott?"

"Yeah!" Mae Mae said, with a puzzled look. "What kind o' business you got with me? Don't too many White folks be comin' into Eastend knockin' on Colored folk's doors."

"Yes, as I was saying. I'm here as a bearer of good news. A lady by the name of Letty Brown apparently thought a lot of you. She had some high paying insurance policies. And the good news is, she names you the beneficiary for them all. That means mam, an accidental death policy, and a policy on her house that burned down, both named you to receive the money."

"I could tell something was botherin' Mama that night after that man left. She kept sayin' something about "death money." She said, takin' money because somebody you love die, jus' ain't right."

"Then the next morning Mama told me what Ma Letty said in a dream. She said Ma Letty came to her laughin' that laugh, talkin' about, 'Girl you git yo'self that café you always been wantin'. Don't you be worryin' about me. It was my time, Chile. You have yo' café. An you have yo'self a good life.'

"God! I loved singin' with that juke box in Mama's place," Esther thought aloud. "I think that's what made me want to be a singer. But Mama didn't want me singin' nothin' but gospel. She was fine as long as I was singin' in the church.

"Mitch, he was always comin' in there wantin' to hear me sing. He was always talkin' about how he

A. Jean Jackson

could make me a star."

Crushing out her cigarette, she rose and answered the tapping at her door. "Speak of the devil," she said laughing. "Yeah Mitch, what's up."

"They're sayin' you might be able to make a record soon. I wanted this song in yo' hands as soon as possible."

"I'm scared Mitch," she said, lighting another cigarette. "I know one thing. I'm doin' it under another name."

"Girl, I don't care if you call yo'self "Mammy". Bein' yo' manager ain't easy. Since you determined you ain't never gone never give me no pussy, I'm ready for this stuff to pay off," he said laughing.

"Mitch, I left Asheville with you because you said you could help me become a star. You know I'll always love Frank."

"I ain't never gone give up, Esther. Frank Jordan ain't never done shit for you. Besides you left Asheville so fast, it didn't seem to matter if you was leavin' Frank or nobody else around there. You was 'bout eighteen and almost finishin' High School. It was round 'bout '43 then. God I can't believe it's 1950 now. But I remember jus' like it was yesterday..."

"Mitch, everything alright here," Mae Mae asked, as she passed by his table. "I see you got the special tonight,"

"Yeah, Mizz Mae, everything jus' lovely," he replied, smiling, showing his gold teeth right in the front of his mouth.

Black-Eyed Peas and Cornbread

Big hands reached across the table and grabbed the salt and pepper shakers. Mae Mae watched his tall frame cry out for more room, as Mitch appeared to be stuffed into the small booth. Though it was tight, it was the booth he always chose. From that booth he had the best view of his Chevy waiting on the outside.

His high yellow light skin, slicked back processed hair and shiny green silk suit seemed to light up the whole café. You could always depend on Mitch eating at Mae Mae's and running the numbers for Eastend.

"You think somebody can bring me a little hot sauce, for these peas, Mizz Mae," Mitch said, after he took his first bite.

"Mildred!" Mae Mae shouted to the waitress in the back. "Stop tryin' to be cute around here, an git some hot sauce for Mitch. Ya'll know what he like. I don't know why in the world you don't jus' bring it when you serve his food."

"Come on. Sit down with me an have some of these blackeyed peas Mizz Mae," Mitch said. "You work too hard. You need to relax sometime an enjoy some of yo' own cookin'."

"Thank you Mitch," she said. "I can cook 'em as good as anybody. But I don't never touch 'em myself. I ain't ate no blackeyed peas in years."

She walked away from Mitch's table swallowing down the spit causing the lump in her throat. Just the thought of blackeyed peas and cornbread, made her sick to her stomach.

A. Jean Jackson

The back door squeaked open as Mildred scurried out. As she left the kitchen Maude came in.

"Maude, what you doin' comin' in here in yo' housecoat and bedroom shoes?" Jimmie asked, as she entered the kitchen through the back door.

"Oh honey, you know I was jus' getting' in from work," she said. "I was tired as hell. Done worked all day long in that white lady's house, cleanin' her toilets, an her children's behins'."

"Anyway," she continued. "I was gone go to bed without eatin' supper. But honey, that fried fish in the air was jus' callin' me. I had to come in here an get me one o' them fried fish sandwiches.

"Where Mizz Mae? I want to holler at her right quick."

"I think she back in the dinin' room," Jimmie said. "You know that woman be all over the place. I can't keep up with her."

When Maude found Mae Mae, she was standing over Jake Daddy pouring water into the empty glass on his table. "Hey Mizz Mae," Maude shouted, grinning widely. "I been lookin' all over this place for you. Honey, you a hard woman to fin'."

"Yeah Maude, what you want?" Mae Mae said, not really wanting to be bothered.

"Girl! I was passin' by yo' house on my way home from work tonight. Jus' seem like to me somethin' wasn't right. I could hear that boy, Elijah shoutin' all the way on the outside. He was mighty loud. Seem real upset at Esther about somethin'.

157

Black-Eyed Peas and Cornbread

"He peeped out an saw me an kind o' settled down. So I figured everything was alright. But I thought I better tell you anyhow."

"You know my children fight all the time," Mae Mae responded, as if she didn't care. "I don't know what I'm gone do with that boy. But thanks for tellin' me."

Mae Mae never looked in Maude's direction. But she watched her depart through the corner of her eye as a strange uneasiness danced in the pit of her stomach.

When business slowed down and most of her customers had left, she secretly rejoiced. The anxiety that Maude left floating arounf her was still there.

"Night Mitch," Mae Mae said, passing by him going towards the double doors.

"Night Mizz Mae," he said. "What's wrong? You look like you got somethin' on yo' mind."

"I don't know, Mitch. I'm jus' kind of worried, that's all. Those children of mine jus' keep me upset all the time."

"Mizz Mae, Elijah ain't never been right," Mitch said, laughing. "But I guess that ain't none of my business. Now Esther. That's a real talented girl. I keep tellin' you I know some people in New York that would love to make her a star."

"That chile too young, Mitch. She was blessed with a good voice. But that's for praisin' the Lord. Her voice wasn't meant for sangin' that hip shakin', body grindin' stuff you talkin' 'bout."

Mitch shook his head and chuckled as Mae

A. Jean Jackson

Mae walked through the double doors of the café. His gold teeth glistened as he opened his mouth to say goodnight. Two days later both he and Esther were gone...

He sat on the bed with Esther and peeped out at the final drizzles of rain. Both of them were silent. Thoughts of where they came from and where they were going played over and over in their heads.

"How about Queen?" You know Queen! Like Queen Esther from the bible. That's what we'll call you!" Mitch said, breaking through their silence.

"Damn, Mitch," Esther said. "Where you get that name. Seem like I remember Mama gave me the name Esther because o' some queen story in the Bible.

"But I don't care. As long as nobody finds out it's really me."

"No way baby! It's perfect. You gone be known as Queen. One word. Queen."

"Alright! Let's do it! Where's that song?"

"Right here," he said, handing her the ruffled papers. "It's jus' right for you. I can hear you singin' it now."

"Anyway, I got to do some runnin' around before the show tonight. I'll be back to pick you up later. You gone give me a goodbye kiss?" he said, smiling devilishly.

"Hell no!" she said, smiling the smile he loved to see.

"I guess after all this time you still savin' them

kisses for Frank," he said, as he departed.

"Yeah Mitch! Don't I wish," Esther said, climbing back under the covers with the song sheets in her hands. "You'd never believe me and Frank only kissed one time in our whole lives," she whispered, as if Mitch were still in the room.

Chapter 13

Stephens Lee High School, "The Castle on the Hill" took her into its bosom like it had always awaited her arrival. But the first thing she saw when she entered the doors was his beautiful smile.

The moment she saw him, she forgot about how old her clothes were. His eyes and his calm friendly manner made everything alright.

"Hello," he said, showing off the deepness of his voice.

"Hey" She said, looking down at the floor.

"This your first year at Stephens Lee?"

"Yeah."

"Welcome. I hope you like it. Maybe I'll see you later."

Esther walked away, pretending that she knew which way to go. When she finally found her way to English class, she walked in and slid into her seat. She looked side-to-side then straight to the back. "Oh God!" she thought to herself, as she jerked around. "It's him!"

His smile met her again as he waited for her outside of the door when the class ended. She blushed as she tried to walk past him.

"Hey! Hey! Wait a minute!" he said, reaching for her arm. "I guess I should've told you. This is my first year too."

"Oh it is," she said, relaxing a little more. "So I guess I'm gone be seein' a lot o' you."

"I hope so," he said, flirting. "Can I walk you

home?"

They walked home that day and everyday until they were juniors in high school. Frank became her friend, her heart, her soul. He became the love of her life. They became the usual occupants of the booth in the back of the cafe.

"Frank you better not be carvin' nothin' on top o' Mama's booth," Esther said, giggling.

"Why not!" He said. "If she see it, then she'll know how much I love you."

"Don't be talkin' like that boy," Esther said, as she watched him forming the letters E.R. love F.J. on the top of the booth. "Mama gone kill you boy. You know I had a hard time gittin' her to let you come here this much.

"An don't be lookin' at me like that," she said, unable to contain her smile. "You lookin' like you want to do somethin' nasty."

"But you know I'm a good lil' Catholic boy. It's a sin for me to have dirty thoughts, like wantin' yo' body," he said, laughing.

Esther could feel her mother's eye on them as they jitterbugged to Fats Domino. Mae Mae was watching, and so was Mitch, as he sat at the bar sipping his beer.

They slow danced on the next song, even though Esther was the taller of the two. It never mattered to her. She couldn't resist his coffee brown complexion, his big dreamy eyes, and his soft dark, curly hair.

As they danced, Frank asked the question he

had always wanted to know. He whispered in her ear as the heat form his breath created a wonderful feeling that ascended her body. His voice was low but she heard him clearly. "Can I kiss you?" he asked softly.

"Next time we walk together from school, I really want to really kiss you," he said. "Not just one of those pecks either. I want a French kiss. I want it to be special."

The next day couldn't come fast enough as Esther waited anxiously on the steps after school. The French kiss, the next step in the progression of their romance had been on her mind all day. She had never kissed that way with anyone before. Preacha had tried, but to her that time in her life didn't matter. That was a time she was trying to forget. But this was the day she had promised Frank they would French kiss.

On the remote dusty road, down the hill from Stephens Lee, Frank stood in front of her. Both of them were nervous, their hands shook as he pecked her lightly on the lips then gently inserted his tongue. He looked deeply into her eyes, then pulled her close and held her tightly in his arms.

Frank's hands searched for the warmth emerging from all parts of Esther's body. Their brains told them to stop but their bodies needed to finish the journey. She grabbed his hand wanting him to stop yet needing him to continue. With a final peck on the lips, Frank withdrew from their embrace.

That afternoon he didn't come into the café. He

led her to the door, said goodbye and walked away. Now, before he did anything else, he needed to make his confession.

"Bless me Father for I have sinned," Frank whispered through the partition in the confessional. "I accuse myself of indecent thoughts and indecent actions.

"Father, I have a girl that I love very much. I want the best for her, and for me. But Father sometimes I want her so bad I almost can't stop myself. The more I'm around her. The more I want her."

"My son," Father Ryan said. "You are a good person. The very fact that you seek help before you give in to your desires, tells me a lot.

"Young men your age will have natural feelings like those you mention. These feelings are simply to test your love for God. So far you have passed the test. Just keep praying. Keep asking for special blessings.

"For your penance say five Hail Marys and five Our Fathers. I would suggest that you try to avoid being alone with your girl."

The 1943 school year ended and gave way to a miserably hot summer. After busy days of helping out in the café, all Esther wanted to do was to lay down and let the mountain air sink into every pore of her body.

The phonograph was on, playing Lady Day.

A. Jean Jackson

Esther watched the curtains blow in the breeze as if it was slow dancing to the music. She listened as she invited the comfort of the cool breeze by stripping down to her slip. With her eyes closed, she laid on the bed and thought of Frank.

Everything was quiet, as she dozed off to sleep. The peacefulness, the music filling the room was just what she needed to escape. Moments later the quiet ended abruptly with a loud thud on the door.

"I saw you doin' it with Frank down on Dirty Eagle Street," Elijah shouted, forcing himself into the room.

His breath smelled like whiskey. Esther knew that whenever he snuck into Mae Mae's whiskey, he was more unbearable than usual. At sixteen, he already drank too much and what he drank, he couldn't control.

"Elijah! Elijah! What's wrong?" she asked, surprised by his sudden intrusion. "Get out of here you drunk! And anyway it ain't none of yo' business what I did with Frank."

"Who you tellin' to get out, Bitch, he said staggering towards her. "I'll beat yo' ass. Anyway, I been waitin' all my life to give you a good beatin'. Mama like you the best. Well, let's see how much she like you after I'm finished with you."

"Gone now, Elijah! leave me alone," she said nervously.

"Tell you what," he said with a smile that highlighted his evil eyes. "Just leave here. Just disappear like you was never born and I'll leave you alone. If you don't, I'll tell Mama and everybody in Eastend what you was doin' all along with Preacha. If you don't, I'll tell her I heard you say you was likin' what Preacha was doing to you. I'll make you out to be the biggest whore in Eastend. Yeah! I'll fix you if you don't leave."

Though the room was dark, all she could see were his dreadful light brown eyes. Deep down behind those eyes, she could see his hate. She could see his pain. She could see that all he ever wanted to do was to destroy her.

"I knew I couldn't never look Mama or those Eastend folks in the eye again. I knew that things between me and Frank would never be the same if he and everybody found out about Preacha.

"But I had to prove I could be somebody. I prayed that Mitch was right...That I could be a star."

Tears ran down Esther's cheeks as she looked out at the clearing New York rain. She held firmly to the crumpled music sheets in her hand. And she wanted to sing. Singing was the only thing that ever helped to take away her pain.

The eyes of strangers stared back at her through the darkness in the room. The only light in the entire room was on her. It caressed her skin, highlighting the beautiful copper tones. It made all who watched her fall in love.

Mitch watched her from the bar. He memorized her every move, her every gesture. He touched her in the only way she would allow...With his eyes.

The room was buzzing with excitement. Smoke circled above like clouds filling, waiting to burst. The anticipation grew as each person waited for her first note.

"You know," she said, in her sexiest voice. "It may be rainin' outside. But I can already tell. Ya'll ready to see some sunshine in here."

She threw her head way back captivating the crowd with the laugh that followed. It left Mitch yearning for her. He wanted to have as much of her as she always gave her audience.

The spotlight went low and the blue tones reflected in her eyes. And for the moments she sang, she took the people inside of her. The last slow, sad song she sang came from her soul. The applause rang in her ears like it would go on forever. But when it stopped, the lonely silence that came always made her think of home.

"That was wonderful," Mitch said, as he entered the dressing room. "They loved you baby. They loved you. Didn't I tell you? Didn't I tell you, I was gone make you a star."

"Mitch," Esther said, looking at him from the mirror. "They jus' give me what I earn, that's all. All the love, all the praise, I work damn hard for it.

"You know when I use to sing gospel songs in church. Even with all o' those people sittin' there in front o' me, I was only singin' for myself an for God. I didn't even give a shit who was listenin', or if they liked it or not. I was jus' praisin' God.

Black-Eyed Peas and Cornbread

"Out here Mitch it's different. Everything is about pleasin' other people. It's about money, an bookins', and when the record is comin' out.

"I ain't sayin' I don't like all o' that. Sometimes that's the only reason I got for getting out o' bed. But sometimes I miss singin' jus' for singin'. Sometimes I miss sharin' my soul with God and nobody else.

"You sound like Mizz Mae now. They say the older women git, the more they act like their own mamas. Mizz Mae use to say yo' voice wasn't supposed to do nothin' but praise the Lord.

"I use to think that was such a damn waste," he said. "I knew the whole world needed to hear yo' voice. And that wasn't gone happen with you just singin' in Eastend in the church.

"You remember singin' at St. James, Esther?" Mitch asked, smiling at her. "You remember how good you was even when you was a little girl?"

"Yeah Mitch. Yeah, I remember," she said, smiling back at him...

"I could jus' barely hear Mizz Gussie on the front pew. She was cryin' an shoutin' Amen, over and over again. I kept on singin'...Jus' praisin' the Lord for puttin' somethin' in my heart an soul that could move folks like that.

"Before I could get out the next chorus, Mizz Gussie was in the aisle right beside Clarise. Everybody know Clarise the biggest gossip in Eastend. But they was both raisin' their arms in the air an shaken like the Holy Ghost was ridin' their backs.

A. Jean Jackson

"When I glanced at Mama, she had this look on her face like my singin', my gift that God gave me, was gone help save her soul. I never knew what it was. But her eyes always looked like she was needin' to be saved from somethin' awful bad.

"Mitch was always sittin' way back in the back o' the church. I could barely see him. But I knew he was there. He was always there when he knew I was gone be singin'.

"He wasn't interested in bein' saved or nothin' like that. Not really. No, Mitch was there for somethin' that didn't have nothin' to do with God.

"His eyes was closed all the while I was singin'. He could see the notes like I was finger paintin' 'em in the air. The high notes, the low notes, even the pauses was dancin' in his head. Mitch can see music. He got a eye for it.

"An Preacha…Ole Preacha. I don't know what that man was hearin' when I sang. But the devil must've been invitin' him right into hell every time he looked at me. Still, he was grinnin' like the proud stepfather.

"That grinnin' fooled me jus' like everybody else. It was enough to make me trus' him. It was enough for him to talk me into takin' my clothes off and gittin' in his bed. An before I even knew what was happenin', that ole man had took away my virginity.

"I thought Mama was gone kill him. After she foun' out about it, her eyes had this distant look. It was like she was rememberin' somethin' from way back.

Black-Eyed Peas and Cornbread

"I know if I hadn't begged her not to, she would've killed him. It's strange how she loved me that much. Lovin' somebody enough to want to kill is a mighty powerful love."

She looked over at Mitch who could tell by her eyes that she was deep in thought. Sadness reflected in the mirror. And Mitch wanted to grab her and make it disappear.

He moved to the back of her as she still faced the mirror. His hands gently massaged her neck and shoulders. "What you thinkin' about now girl," he said, looking into the mirror at her eyes.

"Nothin'," she said, wanting to be held by him, by anyone.

His hands touched her, transferring a warmth that traveled through her whole body. Both of them closed their eyes. They wanted something of each other at that moment that they never knew was possible. It was what he always dreamed of but what she desperately needed.

Esther turned away from the mirror and held on to Mitch like she was holding on for her life. In the heat of passion they kissed and they made love with an urgency that filled the room and took them captive.

Chapter 14

With shaky hands, Elijah reached for his glass of whiskey. Just traces of the light brown liquid covered the ice. But he still turned it up hoping to drain enough to quench his thirst.

"Give me another one, John," he said, tapping the bar.

"You got some more money, Man?" John asked.

"Come on Man. Ain't you always got yo' money from me."

"Yeah. But last time you was short, you had to go beggin' yo' Mama for what you owed me. I ain't gone be waitin' for my money this time."

"I ain't askin' my Mama for nothin' else," Elijah said, digging into his pocket and pulling out a wad of wrinkled bills. "I couldn't never do nothin' to make that woman love me. Nothin'.

"I'm dyin', Man," he said, slurring his words. "An I bet her ass wouldn't even give a shit if she knew."

"What you talkin' about Elijah, with yo' drunk ass?" John asked, with a chuckle. "Yo' black ass ain't no more dyin' than me."

"Yeah Man, I am," Elijah said with sadness in his eyes. "I swear I wouldn't be lyin' about nothin' like that. The doctor say I ain't got long to live. He sayin' I got some kind o' cancer eatin up my body."

"You drink too much Elijah. You shouldn't be drinkin' nothin' now. Not if you that sick."

Black-Eyed Peas and Cornbread

"I know, Man. But I can't help it. You wouldn't believe all the shit I got on my min'. I'm dyin', an drinkin' help me forget.

"When I'm drunk, I ain't got to think about none o' the stuff I'm sorry for. I don't think about my Mama. I don't think about Ma Letty or Preacha. I don't think about Esther. It helps me escape from all o' that."

"Yeah man. But you don't wanna die like that. You need to make yo' peace man, or you gone be sorry. Don't wait 'till it's too late."

"You jus' don't know, John. The things I done, Man I'm goin' straight to hell."

"Jus' go see yo' Mama, Man. Go see Mizz Mae. Tell her what's in yo' heart..."

"She don't care, Man. I seen it all. Even when I was a baby, I seen it all," he said with tears flooding his eyes...

He was fast asleep when he felt her hand on his shoulder. He was just three years old, but the way she shook him, the trembling, the sweaty hand, her urgent manner let him know something was dreadfully wrong.

Rubbing the sleep from his eyes, Elijah rose to the rapid beating in his chest. The look on her face frightened him as he tried to follow her quiet frantic directions. She dressed him quickly. He prepared for an unknown journey as he witnessed pure panic in his mother's face.

Red sat staring, stone cold and rigid as Elijah passed him. He sat not moving, not speaking, seated in the same chair, the same position as the night before.

Though he wondered, Elijah didn't dare ask what was wrong with Red or where they were going. He followed without question as Red's absent stare continued to haunt him on his way out the door.

"Forgive me, Lord! Forgive me! Kept ringing in his ears as Mae Mae repeated it and rushed him out the door. He heard it again and again as he watched her tears fall to the ground in the woods leading from the house.

There were moments when she carried him in her arms close to her chest. Elijah could feel her heart beat. But the heartbeat he felt was not in unison with his own. It was like she had never given him life. It was like he had never developed inside her womb. As close as he was, and as bad as he yearned to feel the love from some unknown corner of her heart, he didn't.

His tiny hands clutched tightly to the warmth and moisture of her slender fingers as she used them to tug him along. But her fingers were absent of any tenderness.

She was compelled by some deep commitment that had nothing to do with him. Her frantic movements and her determination had everything to do with a daughter who awaited her back at Ma Letty's.

Elijah trudged on beside his mother. But he had never been so tired. He wanted to stop. He wanted to sit down. But no matter what he did, she pulled and she carried and she swore at him until she could see the distance grow between them and the house.

"I wish I had never brought yo' ass," she kept saying. "I knowed I was gone be sorry for bringin' you. You holdin' me back boy, jus' like I thought."

Broken pieces of his heart could be seen through his eyes, as he listened to her words and ran faster, trying to keep up. It was as if pleasing her now while she was running for her life, was more important than ever before.

When they were finally through the woods and close to the dirt rocky road, she stopped. Elijah coughed clearing his lungs. Alert eyes moved about watching her, watching his surroundings, as he tried to catch his breath.

"Let's go," she said, after a short moment. "I ain't got time to be slow pokin' around waitin' for you.

They walked for a while then descended the hill that reached out and formed a grassy glade that touched the road. Once again she stopped. But this time she listened.

"What's that?" she asked, turning her ear towards the road. "Listen!"

Elijah stopped. He looked left and right, hoping that whatever it was she wanted to be there, would be.

A brief moment later an old pick-up rounded the curve. Elijah could tell by Mae Mae's excitement as well as the nervous twitch in her hand that something exciting was about to happen.

A. Jean Jackson

"Mornin' sir." She said, looking down at the ground beside the truck.

"What in the hell you doin' jumpin' in front o' my truck, Gal," the young man said, showing his irritation. I could've jus' kept right on goin' over yo' black ass. Far as I'm concerned, you'd be one less nigga in the worl'."

Elijah stared in silence spellbound by the strange way his mother was acting. He stood behind his mother's tall thin frame and peeped at the man. He didn't want to be seen but tried not to miss a word.

"Yessir," he heard his mother say, as she still looked at the ground. "I'm sorry for stoppin' you like that. I don't mean no harm. My boy here an me, we would give anything to be able to git a ride with you.

"Ain't that many folks ridin' through this way sir. An my boy, he young an he real tired," Mae Mae said, pushing Elijah to the front of her.

"Hell, I don't be ridin' no niggas, gal," he said, getting out of the truck and spitting at the side of the road. "But tell you what. You give me some o' that deep down nigga pussy, I'll let you ride."

Elijah saw his mother's expression suddenly change. "Sir," she said, with a weak nervous laugh. "I know you got to be in a big hurry. An I ain't wantin' to hold you up none.

"I got me a lil' money from workin' in Mizz Harris' house," she said, pulling it out, showing him a wad of bills. "You can have it, Sir. You can have it all. Jus' please! Please help us."

The man reached out and grabbed the handful

of bills. He counted the money and looked back and forth from his hand to the two of them.

"Gone git in the back, then," he said, tucking the bills into his pocket. "You got to ride in the back. An before we pulls into town, ya'll got to git out an walk. You hear?"

"Yessir," she said, rushing to put Elijah on the back of the truck. "Long as we ridin', we don't care what end of the truck we on."

Elijah watched the dignity return to his mother's face as they bounced and jerked from the truck's movement on the bumpy road. They rode together for miles and she didn't speak. The far off look in his mother's eyes told Elijah that she was riding with him, but her mind was somewhere else...

When they arrived at Ma Letty's house. The strangers in the room made Elijah not want to leave Mae Mae's side. He held on tight but her grip loosened as she left him and ran towards the girl.

With a joy and excitement in Mae Mae's face that Elijah had never witnessed before, he watched as she grabbed the little girl. Elijah smiled covering the fact that he felt all alone in the world.

He stood alone in the middle of Ma Letty's floor and he envied the smiles, the hugs, and the kisses that Mae Mae gave so easily. He saw the love that he'd never received given to this strange girl, and immediately he hated her.

"Esther baby! My precious baby! I missed you so much!" Mae Mae said, with tears in her eyes. "You remember me, Esther? Chile, I'm yo' Mama. I know I been gone over three years. But I had to go with Mr. Red. I didn't want to go. I never wanted to leave you."

The two children, the sister and brother, stared at each other. They looked nothing alike. Elijah with his freckled face, looked at her through eyes that were just like Reds. And Esther with her beautiful carved features and the dark deep eyes of Jacob, looked back at him...

Elijah finished his drink by turning it up and flinching from the stinging it caused in his chest. He closed his eyes, took a deep bre'ath and held it.

"Listen John!" he said, pointing at the jukebox, stopping all movement in the bar. "You know who that sound like, Man?"

"No. Who?"

"It's Esther! My God in heaven, it's Esther!"

As he listened a single tear dropped from his eye. Though the label that showed through the window of the jukebox read, "Strange Kind o' Love" by Queen, he knew it was her.

His tears were falling fast and furious yet Elijah had no idea where they were coming from. He tried to hide them by wiping his eyes and nose with the back of his hand. He hadn't cried in a very long time. But he knew he needed these to cleanse his soul.

"Esther had dreams," Elijah thought, as he listened to her voice. "She dreamed she was gone be a real singer. An it look like she made it.

"I hated her. I was jealous of her. I wanted her

to feel jus' like Mama always made me feel. I wanted her to think nobody loved her either. I sent her away like that 'cause I wanted to hurt her like Preacha did. I wanted her to feel the same kind of loneliness and pain I felt from the day I was born. I was glad when Preacha hurt her. It didn't matter that Preacha never gave me the time of day. Whether I fit in or not, that was the only real family I knew..."

As he looked at the smiles that covered the faces of everyone seated at the dinner table, a feeling of warmth touched his heart. Though he never expressed it, the idea of being part of a family in Preacha's house made Elijah very happy.

He watched Preacha's mouth, not hearing a word of the grace he offered for the meal. But Elijah was happy a blessing was being offered. It made it more like a "family."

"We thank you, Lord God in heaven for the food," Preacha said, as Elijah sighed, thinking the blessing would never end. "Bless the food we are about to receive. An Bless Mae Mae for preparin' somethin' so special for us. Bless us in Christ's name. Amen."

Everything seemed to be in slow motion as Elijah took a big bite from his fried chicken. It was like his life was so perfect, that it was moving slow enough for him to try to enjoy it.

As the days passed, a picture of his family was being painted right before his eyes. It was a picture that he wanted to carry with him forever.

A. Jean Jackson

He liked to think of Preacha sitting at his desk planning how to bring deliverance to the worst souls in Eastend. Saturdays were Preacha's time for finding the perfect words, the perfect gestures for herding the flock of poor lost sheep a little closer to heaven on Sunday mornings.

Even Esther was a part of Elijah's special family picture. She was always busy dusting and cleaning; doing something, anything. She had a need to be the perfect child. And the more perfect Esther acted, the more Elijah hated her. Her perfection was his excuse for hating her.

The happy sound of his mother humming as she worked was the most glorious sound on earth. To Elijah, it made his family picture complete. He needed that sound to replace the love she never gave him.

Eyes that Mae Mae never knew were watching followed the movement of her hands as she hung clothes on the line. One by one each piece went up on the line. Clothes hanging clean and white on the line helped Elijah know that things were perfect.

The perfection reflected in Mae Mae's face. Seeing that look, that peace that had always been missing before, brought Elijah unbelievable happiness.

Then as swiftly as it began, the slow motion of Elijah's happy life changed to a whirlwind of chaotic disaster. The dream ended before he knew it was over. The peace, the perfection, the homelife inside Preacha's world would never be his again.

"I'll kill you ole man," he heard his mother say

to Preacha. "You done gone an messed with my lil' angel."

After a while, the sounds were muffled. Whatever was being said, Elijah could no longer hear it. He moved away from the door and towards the kitchen.

"Mama talkin' about she gone kill Preacha," he said to Esther, sensing the unraveling of his perfect life. "It's all 'cause o' you too. Whatever Preacha did, you should've jus' kept it to yo' self. You done ruined everything. Now we got to go back an live with Ma Letty."

Cold eyes stared at Esther, though they didn't see her. They didn't see the person inside. They didn't see the hurting girl who had just been raped by the man posing as "a man of God."

The day ended as they left Preacha seated at his desk looking out of the window. A coldness recaptured Elijah's heart as he looked back towards Preacha.

Mae Mae's peaceful, happy face was gone. "I'll kill you," she kept saying over her shoulder. "You hear me! You hurt my baby girl again. You gone wish you was dead."

Her words, her tone, the expression on her face was from another far off evil time in his life. It was a reminder of the day they slid and fell and climbed out of Hell and away from Red. And Elijah had hoped to never see again...

"I ain't gone never forget that look on

A. Jean Jackson

Preacha's face, long as I live," Elijah said, putting another nickel into the jukebox. "An all the way to Ma Letty's, I was blamin' Esther for messin' up my life.

"I was hurtin' too much to think about how much Preacha hurt her. I didn't care. Then, I jus' couldn't see it."

Chapter 15

He searched all of the eyes that stared at him as he entered the café. But the only eyes he wanted to see were his mother's. Mae Mae was the one he so desperately needed to see.

"Over here boy," she said from a dark corner of the café. "I guess you lookin' for me ain't you?"

"Yeah Mama," Elijah said. "I need to talk to you."

"What in the hell you want now, boy?" she said, with her hands on her hips.

"Jus' listen for a minute, Mama. That's all I'm askin. There's somethin' I really want you to hear."

He walked over to the jukebox and stood for a moment. To keep his balance he held on, then he punched his selection.

"Strange Kind o' Love", by Queen, circled through the jukebox as the arm placed it precisely on the turntable. Elijah paused then sat down in the booth near his mother.

"Mama, you know who that is?" he asked, as Mae Mae sat down.

"Listen. Listen real close."

"That's somebody named Queen or somethin' like that," she answered.

"People in that business sometimes change their names, Mama. That's Esther. I know it! It ain't nobody but her!"

Mae Mae listened intently for a long moment. She closed her eyes then looked back at Elijah. "My

A. Jean Jackson

God! It is her! Where on earth is she? Where is my baby girl?"

The record played on as Mae Mae and Elijah looked at each other. With each word of the song rising softly into the air, anger rose in Mae Mae's face. "What you care about it anyway, Elijah! You always hated Esther!

"I could never prove it. But I know you had somethin' to do with her leavin'. After all these years, why you ain't man enough to say it?"

"I ain't happy about none o' the stuff I done, Mama!" Elijah screamed. "Yeah! I made Esther leave. I told her she wasn't never gone be nothing'. I even told her I was gone tell lies about her and Preacha.

"I was mad at everybody in the world, especially you. I hated the way you loved her so much, an you didn't love me."

Anger and sadness filled the room and surrounded both of them. All eyes and ears turned to their corner of the café. Their lives played out along with the sounds of Esther's voice rising from the jukebox. All of Eastend was listening.

Mae Mae's face was on fire. Elijah looked more like Red today than he ever had before in her life. She blinked, wishing he would just disappear.

Elijah's words blinded her. Mae Mae reached for his throat but stopped short and grabbed his collar. She stood and pulled him up out of his seat. Her hand pulled back to strike him.

Embarrassment crossed Elijah's face as he raised his hands just in time to block his face. He grabbed her wrists and gently lowered her back into her seat.

Elijah looked about the room and looked into the eyes of the people watching. He softened his tone so that only he and Mae Mae could hear what was being said.

"Mama, I ain't never wanted to hurt you," he said, almost in a whisper. "No matter what else was goin' on in this family, I always adored you. All I ever wanted was for you to love me."

"Love you! Elijah, I feel like killin' you. I feel like I could take my bare hands and take away the very life I gave you. And don't think it won't happen. You better look over yo' shoulder for the rest of yo' life."

"I'm askin' you to forgive me. If you can't, I understand. I jus' need to get it all out. I jus' need to tell you all the things I did."

His light brown eyes were even lighter as they filled up with tears. A dark shadow formed on his face that revealed a look of utter regret and defeat. His next revelation came from deep down in his gut like he was being forced to throw it up.

"I killed Ma Letty, Mama!" he said, sobbing. That fire that burned her up. I set it. But I swear, I tried to put it out before it caught. I swear. When I went to sleep that night, I thought it was out…"

The walk on Dirty Eagle was lonely as Elijah returned home from school. Rocks and dust scattered as he kicked with each step he took. He hated where he was coming from and he hated where he was going. To Elijah, both school and home were two worlds he couldn't wait to escape.

The slamming of the door could be heard all over the house when he arrived home. "What's wrong wit' him?" Mae Mae asked, after she'd inquired about his day at school.

"I don't know, Chile," said Ma Letty. "Seem like he mad at the world all the time. He ain't been right since ya'll left Preacha's. Maybe I can talk to him later. I know most times he stay so mad at you, he can't hear nothin' you say."

"OK, Ma. We got to do somethin' about that boy. He messin' up in school everyday. On top o' that, he can't stand nobody's guts in this whole house."

Later in the evening, Ma Letty talked and Elijah pretended to listen. All the while he was plotting how he would destroy all of them.

He took the wooden matches and lit them one at a time. Each time, each one he lit, he watched until the flames died down to nothing at all. There was something magical about fire. Fire was everything. It was good, it was bad. Fire could warm you or it could burn you. It was beautiful yet it was powerful and destructive.

"That ole sick ass lady tryin' to tell me what to do," he said to himself. "She come callin' me into her room talkin' about how I better change. Talkin' about if I don't, how somethin' awful bad gone happen to me.

"All she can say is how much my Mama love me. But I know that's a bunch of shit. Hell! I know my Mama ain't never really loved but one o' her children.

Black-Eyed Peas and Cornbread

An it sho' ain't me. Esther the only one she care anything about. Ma Letty know that. She see it good as anybody.

"Every time something go wrong. They all make out like it's always my fault. They think Esther a angel. But she can't be all that good and pure. Hell! I know Preacha done had some o' her pussy.

"I can't do nothin' unless they be watchin'. It's like they think I'm the devil. It's like they think I'm gone do something awful."

The heat from the flame of his match approached the thumb of his left hand then flickered out. He rolled over onto his back and closed his eyes. "Yeah, they think I'm so bad. I'm gone show 'em how bad I can be."

When it was dark and everything was quiet, he tipped through the house. He paused for a moment, peeping into Ma Letty's room. A certain auora of peacefulness surrounded the two women as Mae Mae dozed seated beside Ma Letty's bed.

The vision stayed with him as he moved away, heading for the cramped dirty space under the house. He knelt down and lit another match. The light from it highlighted the spider webs and the bugs scattered all about him.

"I'm gone do it," he said to himself. "I ain't even scared. I hate all of 'em. I don't even care if they all burn alive."

One by one all of his matches burned away in his hand. As the flames remaining on the last match moved closer to his fingers, he dropped it. The flames fell as if to their death, then revived as they hit the straw of an old discarded broom.

Elijah smiled as he looked down at the magic of the white ghostly smoke suddenly bursting into bright beautiful orange flames. His heart pumped faster and faster. Beads of sweat formed on his brow.

"No!" exploded in his head, as he stood and stamped out the flames. "I can't. I thought I could. But I can't."

A feeling of disappointment captured him as he stood and walked away. As he passed Ma Letty's room this time he breathed a sigh of relief. "I couldn't do it," he said to himself, looking at the dozing women. "I jus' couldn't do it."

He climbed into bed and he laid awake until he heard Mae Mae returning to her room. He tossed and turned, waiting for the sleep that finally came.

"Boy you better change yo' ways," he heard Ma Letty say to him in his dream. "Change before it's too late," she said.

Her voice was clear. It was like she was standing right there over his bed. He could see her sweating and straining, trying to take him by the hand. But Elijah turned his head. He refused to reach out his hand.

"Fire! Fire! Everybody out," Elijah heard, as he jumped awake. "Wake up everybody! You got to get out!" he heard his mother shriek.

He sat up in bed trying to separate reality from the dream. Before he knew it, he was outside facing flames that were lighting up the evening sky.

Black-Eyed Peas and Cornbread

The flames reflecting in his mother's tearful eyes magnified the sadness he saw. It was the same look that had been there many times before. But this time he knew he was the cause of it. He knew it was his fault that Ma Letty couldn't be saved from the fire.

An though Elijah knew Ma Letty was dead. The fire, the pure essence of the flames at their peak in both beauty and destruction, brought a smile to his face that he could not control. It was the most beautiful sight that Elijah had ever seen...

Mae Mae rose abruptly with the silencing of the jukebox. Elijah was scared of the emotions he had stirred in her. But he met her stare directly.

Mae Mae's mouth trembled as she spoke. "I always knowed you wasn't nothin' but the devil. I always knowed you was jus' like yo' Daddy," she screamed, as her whole body shook.

"You look like him. You act like him. Far as I'm concerned you ain't never belonged to nobody but him. I birthed you. But you was never mine.

"God! I still can't believe my ears! I can't believe you set the fire that burned up my Ma Letty! Ain't nobody on this earth never been as good to me as Ma Letty! Nobody!"

Elijah listened as his eyes looked down at the table. He knew he deserved the wrath she lashed at him. But still Mae Mae's words erupted his anger.

"I'm sorry, Mama!" he said. "But I kept lookin' for love from you. That's all, jus' love. An all I ever saw was hate in yo' eyes."

A. Jean Jackson

She slid out of the booth, surprised and silenced by his words. Those things he said, those justifications for his path in life, she simply didn't want to hear.

"Why couldn't you just hurt me, boy? Instead o' goin' around hurtin' all the people I loved. Ma Letty died at yo' hands. An Esther, I ain't knowed nothin' o' her where abouts for over seven years. You took 'em away from me boy. You took both of 'em away."

"Yeah, I know Mama," Elijah said, seeing that things were worse between them now than ever. "But the real problem is, you loved everybody else but me."

The words hung in the air as Elijah turned to leave. She moved closer to him. He could feel the warmth of her breath near his ear. She whispered so that no one else could possibly hear the words she uttered. But still, they rang loudly in his ears.

"By the way," Mae Mae said. "If I ever see yo' sorry ass again, I will kill you."

Tears fell at the forking roads of Mountain and Pine as Elijah walked away. He stopped to cough, as he held his chest and spit along the side of the road.

Loneliness engulfed his heart unlike any other time in his life. And as much as he wanted to, he didn't look back. He never turned and noticed the tearful eyes of his mother following until he disappeared.

Chapter 16

The night train always left the Biltmore station heading north at the same time. Right on time, just like clockwork, at 2:00 in the morning the whistle was blowing, and the train was jerking away.

Elijah approached cautiously pulling the collar of his coat up high around his neck. The mountain air was always chilly this time of morning. Dew had settled on everything, not knowing if the unpredictable temperatures would turn it to frost before the light of morning.

With hands tucked deeply into his empty pockets, he searched for the car he was going to board. To him, they all looked alike in the dark.

Weak and frail he grabbed the long bar attached to the first open door he found. With what felt like his last ounce of strength, he stepped high and pulled himself up.

Moments after his eyes adjusted, he met a faceless stare coming from a dark corner of the car. The eyes glared as if disturbed by his intrusion.

"We don't allow no damn niggas in our car," a voice behind the eyes shouted from the dark.

"I don't want no trouble, Mister," Elijah said, nervously. "I'm jus' a poor old boy wantin' a free ride up north. That's all."

"You hear what I said, boy," the man said, moving closer to Elijah pulling out a knife.

"There a problem here?" a strange voice called out from nowhere. Behind the voice came a dark

A. Jean Jackson

muscular man who jumped up into the car. He was a stranger, but Elijah was glad to see him.

"Mister, he with me," the large Colored man said, grinning, putting his arm around Elijah. "He jus' forgot what car we was on. I'm gone show him which way to go though."

"Yeah Sambo! You do that," the White man said. "This train gone be headin' out soon. An I ain't gone be ridin' with no niggas."

"Come on, man. Come with me," the Colored man said as he pushed Elijah. "I see yo' ass don't know nothin' about hopin' no trains."

Elijah followed behind him like a lost little boy. The man's long strides went swiftly back six cars where he hopped up in one graceful leap. He offered Elijah his hand and pulled him aboard jus' as the train began to jerk away.

Inside the car, five men looked over Elijah, but said nothing. The men had only two things in common. They were all Black and they were all traveling north on the back end of a freight train.

The helpful attitude of the big guy seemed to fade with the movement of the train. It was the way of the hobo. Life for them was basically every man for himself.

Though Elijah was riding with them, he was different from them. He knew where he was going. And he knew why he had to go. The others were riding wherever the train took them. The train's predictable destinations provided the only stability in their lives.

Black-Eyed Peas and Cornbread

Though rules were never stated, Elijah followed the unspoken laws in the car. He could tell everyone wanted their own space. They didn't like a lot of idle talk. And they were proud of traveling alone, yet happy they didn't have to be alone.

The chill that hung about the car grabbed hold of Elijah and refused to let him go. His thin coat was not enough to help him fight the battle, as he pulled it tighter around his body. He was determined to be a man. His thoughts of discomfort had to be forced from his mind.

After a long restless night, the dawn of morning showed through the crack in the door. "Man, what's wrong with you," the dark muscular man said, as he turned over to face Elijah. "You been over there moanin' an groanin' and coughin' like you was about to croak."

"I'm a'right," Elijah said, between coughs. "I been real sick lately, that's all."

"Why you out here on this night train, Man. This ain't no place for no sick man. Up north folks don't give a shit about you. They can watch you die with out blinkin' an eye."

"I got family up there, Man. My sister up in New York. That's who I'm goin' to see."

His thinning sickly face and his disheveled appearance was ignored by the dark lonely eyes surrounding him in the night club. It was like his slow, silent death was normal in this big city. It was like this kind of wasting away was an every day thing.

A. Jean Jackson

Elijah sat in a dark back corner. He smoked and he waited. The room was filled with people who were waiting. They all were waiting for her.

Everyone said she was the most beautiful, talented woman in Harlem. And when she entered the stage from the right and moved gracefully to the stool in the middle, every part of the room lit up.

"Good evening ladies and gentlemen," she said, sipping from a glass of scotch, and captivating the hearts of everyone listening. "I'd like to sing a little bit from my song, "Strange Kind O' Love'.""

A tight fitting sequined white dress, sitting low on her broad, brown shoulders enhanced her beautiful smile. Teeth that were so white they glowed in the dark, flirted with the crowd as she waited for their applause to subside.

The song came from deep down inside her soul. All of her songs were delivered like she was making love to the audience without ever touching them. And 'Strange Kind of Love' was right at the end of their foreplay. It always made them want her more.

Elijah's heart raced as he listened and observed the adoration all over the room. It was hard to imagine just how far Esther had come. But it was clear by glancing about at the smiling crowd, that she had become a star.

Esther gave the audience all she had as Elijah watched proudly. And after the set ended, she stole away to her dressing room to relax. Giving so much of herself took energy. That was evident in the sweat rolling down her face.

Black-Eyed Peas and Cornbread

In the dressing room and away from the loud applause, her loneliness returned. She sat down facing the mirror and tried to see the person that everyone else seemed to love.

"Come on in," she said, acknowledging a soft knock on the door.

"Hello Esther," Elijah said, peeping through the door. "Remember me?"

Esther turned, trying to see if what she saw in the mirror was real. "What you want, Elijah? How'd you find me?" she said, with a look of shock on her face.

"I had to find you, Esther," he said, coming into the room. "I was determined to find you. I need your help. I need your forgiveness. I'm dyin', Esther. I need you to help me save my soul."

"I can't believe you came here."

"Please Esther, jus' let me talk to you for a minute. I came a long way. Please."

"You got one minute," she said forcefully. "Then I want you out of here."

"Esther, go home to see Mama. She miss you. She been missin' you for a long time."

"You tried to destroy me. You caused me to leave Eastend. An you got the nerve to come here tellin' me yo' sad stories. I'll never forget what you did to me. Never!

"Now, get out o' my face, Elijah! I'm sorry you came all this way."

Elijah turned and started back out of the door.

A. Jean Jackson

Before he closed the door, he looked back at Esther. "You know," he said, with tears in his eyes. "Mama ain't never loved me the way she loved you."

She listened to his footsteps until they were silent. Though she knew he was gone, she continued to see his sad, sick face in the mirror...

There was a time when Ma Letty was the only mother Esther knew. And though she missed being close to Mae Mae's warm loving bossom, she was blessed with Ma Letty's special kind of love.

Every night they knelt down beside the bed and prayed for God to bring her Mama back. They prayed for her to be safe and sound. But for three or more years their prayers were never answered.

"My Mama ain't never comin' back, Ma Letty," Esther said. "She must not love me. 'Cause if she loved me she would've come back."

"Chile," Ma Letty said, taking her onto her lap. "If there's a way for yo' Mama to get back. She gone find it. Ain't much in this world gone keep her away from a angel like you. Jus' wait. She comin' back real soon."

Ma Letty touched her heart as she forced herself to lie once again. She was worried about Mae Mae. But she didn't know what to tell Esther. She didn't know where Mae Mae was or what she was doing She didn't even know if she was dead or alive.

What worried Ma Letty most were Esther's dreams. Every night she would go to Esther's beside and find her crying and scared. Ma Letty would wrap the child in her arms to try to stop her from trembling.

"What you see in that dream, Chile," she'd say. "You tell me about it, an I'll take it on."

"I see my Mama," Esther said. "Somebody real mean holdin' her. They big and they got scary eyes. My Mama really wants to leave. She want to come home real bad. But he won't let her.

"She sad an she cryin' an she callin' my name from far, far away. When she reach out for me, that man with the scary eyes always pull her back."

With Ma Letty's big, warm loving arms all around her, Esther always drifted back to sleep. Ma Letty kissed her on the cheek and tucked in the covers and brought the peace back to Esther's face.

"Dreams always mean something," she'd say to herself, as she laid awake waiting for her own sleep to return. "I jus' wish I knew what."

The time that Mae Mae was away seemed like it would never end. The dreams continued but the waiting faded to hopelessness. When they finally gave up and created a life of normalcy without her, Mae Mae returned.

Ma Letty's screams could be heard all over the boarding house. And soon after that scream of joy, the tall woman who looked like Esther's vague memory of her mother, grabbed her screaming and crying.

When Mae Mae released Esther, she saw the boy. He stared at her as if he hated her. And as their eyes connected, fear jolted her heart. The boy's light brown scary eyes were just like the ones she'd seen

A. Jean Jackson

in her dreams…

"Good show!" Mitch shouted, as he entered the dressing room. "Baby! I think you get better and better."

"Mitch, Elijah was jus' here," Esther said, with a shaky voice.

"You alright baby? What he say? What he want?"

"He's different, Mitch," she said thoughtfully. "He wasn't like he was before. He said he dyin' and he want me to forgive him. He sayin' Mama misses me, and that I should go home.

"She did love me more, Mitch," Esther said, with tears filling her eyes. "I could tell the first time I saw him. I could tell she didn't love him.

"Is that what made him a monster, Mitch? Is that what made him hate everybody and everything?"

"I don't know, Esther," Mitch answered, thoughtfully.

"If he dyin' Mitch! Is that supposed to make a difference? Don't every person deserve some peace before they die? If God forgives us, ain't we supposed to try to forgive each other?"

"You ain't God, girl," Mitch said, jokingly. "God can do whatever he want to."

"Mitch this ain't funny," she said, scolding. "It broke my heart when he said he was dyin'. I tried my best not to feel anything. But I did.

"I remember when Mama use to brag about me all the time. An whenever she was braggin' on me she was always puttin' him down. She made me look like the angel. An everything he did was wrong.

"One time for Christmas I got this doll. It was a white doll with long blond hair. But God! I loved that doll. An Elijah knew jus' how much I loved it. Jus' to get on everybody nerves he was always threatenin' to tear that doll up. An Mama, she'd jus' tell him to shut up. She'd say, "You mess with that doll boy, I'm gone whip yo' butt."

Mitch sat down in the chair beside the dresser. He wanted to hear every word. He wanted to be there for her, no matter what.

"Anyhow," she continued. "I'd be playin' an he'd be watchin'. Then he'd go off laughin' like he had a private joke or somethin'.

"One day I was combin' that dolls hair. Well, I jerked the comb jus' a little bit too hard, an that doll's head came right off in the floor. I was so hurt, I ran out o' the house cryin' like it was my head on the floor.

"Mama, jus' saw me cryin'. She didn't see nothin' else. Honey, that's all she needed to see. That woman never liked to see me upset about nothin'.

"She saw that dolls head layin' on the floor. An next thing I know, she had Elijah, beatin' the shit out of him so bad you could hear him hollerin' all over Eastend.

"Sad thing about it, Mitch. She didn't ask no questions. That doll was tore up. An in her mind, Elijah did it. That's the way she thought.

"I finally told Mama that Elijah didn't do it. An you know she never told him she was sorry. She jus' sent him to his room. Elijah was right, Mitch. Mama didn't love him. She never did."

Chapter 17

The familiar sound of his footsteps pounded in her head. Her heart beat faster as each step grew closer. She held her breath and waited, just as she always did. She waited for him.

Turning her head back and forth in search of him, she reached out her hand into the darkness. Feeling nothing, seeing nothing, she could still sense he was there. His horrible smell was already filling the air around her. As much as she hated it, as much as she feared it, he was in the room.

"Mr. Red!" Mae Mae shouted. "That you? Where you come from?"

"From hell! Where you think!" he said, grabbing her by the wrist.

His light brown eyes glared in the darkness, showing the only part of his face that she could see. The heat of his body was close to her. But it was his scary eyes that really confirmed his presence.

"The boy. He dyin'," Red said.

"Who! What boy?" she asked, nervously.

"Elijah. He dyin'. But don't nobody care. You hate him. You always have."

"He my son. I birthed him into this world."

"That don't mean you love him. Do it?" he said, snatching at her hand. "What's the matter, Gal? He look too much like me? That why you hate the boy?"

His question hung in the stale air as Mae Mae jumped awake. And he was gone…

A. Jean Jackson

The slow calm light of dawn was creeping through the window telling her that the night had slipped away. She sat up surprised that her easy chair and not her bed had held her through the night.

Pictures of the young faces of Esther and Elijah looked down at her from the mantle. Their bright but sad eyes renewed her feelings of despair. The pain from it formed a lump in her throat.

"God! I jus' dreamed Elijah was dyin'. What does it mean? What's wrong with me?

"Where'd you go, baby girl?" Mae Mae asked, looking affectionately at Esther's picture.

"Why'd you do all the evil things you done," she said, turning to the picture of Elijah. "Why'd you send yo' own flesh an blood away like that, boy? An why'd you kill Ma Letty?

"I don't know if you dyin', boy. But I swear, jus' like I said, I'll kill you myself. I killed yo' evil Daddy, an I'll kill you too. Anybody that hurts the people I love like that, they don't deserve to live. I ain't never gone understand what on God's earth made you so evil, Elijah?"

Rising slowly, Mae Mae stretched and went towards the kitchen. She approached the stove and put on a pot of coffee. The smell of it signaled that her morning was truly beginning. Once the coffee was on, she grabbed the broom and headed for the front porch.

As she swept, there was a quiet but vigorous rhythm to the movement of the broom. It was a rhythm that Mae Mae had perfected from years of repetition. Sweeping the porch first thing each and every morning was as natural to her as drinking her first cup of coffee.

The dust flying off of the broom was like the questions circling in her mind. The answers were not clear to her. They were hidden somewhere in each scattered particle of dust.

"Damn! That kettle loud," Mae Mae said to herself, as it whistled its readiness, and beckoned her inside. "It scares me every time it starts goin' off."

As the whistling stopped, she poured her cup of coffee and returned to her large stuffed chair. She settled in and listened to the clock on the mantle as it ticked its constant reminder of routine.

There was always something special about her first sip of coffee. She sighed as she slurped from the cool liquid settling in the saucer. The coffee, the smells, the sound of morning, all spoke silently of her loneliness and despair. She poured the contents of the kettle into a large green porcelain basin. Steam rose into the air as she reached in wetting her white washrag. When she finished washing and felt clean to her own satisfaction, she dressed and headed for the café.

"Mornin' Jimmie," said Mae Mae. "You done started them biscuits? You know I like 'em fresh out the oven when the early folks get here."

"Yeah. Yeah, Mizz Mae. I thank I know how to run this kitchen by now."

The white apron that Mae Mae pulled over her

A. Jean Jackson

head seemed to shine in the morning light. She tied it at the back then peeped into the oven door checking Jimmie's biscuits for herself. "Look like they about ready," she said. "Now gone an get them grits on."

"They on Mizz Mae! They on!"

"Well that don't mean yo' ass ought to be sittin' down. I ain't payin' you to be sittin' down this mornin'."

When the song began, Mae Mae went to the booth in the back and touched the initials that were carved into the table.

"Strange Kind o' Love. They say you don't love me an I try to explain. It's strange. It's jus' a strange kin' o' love. Use to beat me, mistreat me. An all I can say. It's strange."

Mae Mae listened intently with her eyes closed. She fought back the tears that threatened to come every time she heard Esther's voice on the jukebox.

"God! What is you tryin' to tell me?" she thought to herself. "What it all mean, Lord?"

The forking streets at Mountain and Pine came together and escorted her to the double doors of the café. She looked over her shoulder at the whole of Eastend. The fur collar on her bright red coat announced her arrival before she turned and walked inside.

Dark, long, black hair, pinned high and tucked under a wide brimmed hat, enhanced her beautiful complexion. Dark penetrating yet thoughtful eyes peeped inside and then entered.

"Hello Mama," she said calmly, as if she had

been gone only a day or so.

"Lord God! Esther! My baby! My precious baby! You came back! You finally came back!" Mae Mae said, as she ran to Esther with open arms.

"Mama! I missed you! I really missed you!" Esther said, sobbing, reaching out to hug her back.

In the silence of their tears they held on tight. Their tears mixed together forming the bond again that had disappeared years before. They kissed and hugged and looked deeply into each other's eyes in hopes of finding the missed years.

"You look good, baby," Mae Mae said, after a long moment. "Come on an sit a spell. "Lord Chile, I thought I wasn't gone never see you no more."

"I know Mama. I just had to get away. So much was happenin' to me here, I jus' couldn't stay."

"I'm mighty proud o' that song o' yours," Mae Mae said, changing the subject. "I see you made it. Jus' like Mitch was sayin'. I can't believe you right there in that juke box, singin' right beside all them other famous folks."

A look of pride rested on Mae Mae's face as she stared at Esther lighting a cigarette. "Mitch been with me all the time, Mama," she said blowing smoke into the air. "We left here together. Now, after all these years we finally gone get married. I'm havin' his baby, Mama."

"Do you love him, Chile?"

"No. But he knows it. He knows that it's not just him. He knows I have a hard time with loving anybody like that. One day I might learn. But Mitch is willin' to wait. He believes in me. He always have."

And as they spoke of him, like a sudden changing of the tide, Mitch entered through the double doors. Esther's eyes greeted his with a familiarity that was known only to them.

"Hey honey," he said, to Esther. "An you, Mizz Mae. I see you still lookin' as good as ever."

"Mitch!" Mae Mae said, glancing at his expensive gray silk suit, and suede shoes. "Welcome home. I hear you about to be part o' the family."

"Oh! I see Esther told you," he said, laughing, showing his gold teeth. "I love her, Mizz Mae. I want you to know that. I always have."

"Well from what I can see, she been mighty blessed."

Mitch sat down with them and glanced at the initials F.J. and E.R. carved onto the booth table top. The letters had been there for close to ten years. "This place is the same," he said smiling, looking at Esther for reassurance. "I drank a many a beer in this place"

They reminisced for a while, sitting in the booth that years before had been occupied by Frank Jordan and Esther Redman. But Esther knew she could not put it off any longer. It was time for her to really go home.

The smell of oldness greeted her at the front door. Time had passed. But everything in her mother's house was still the same. As with everything else in Eastend and in the cafe, nothing had really changed.

Memories were everywhere. The good ones and the bad ones taunted her like laughing ghosts welcoming her home. She walked to the mantle and reached up, giving in to the urge to touch the picture of herself.

A beautiful little girl with missing front teeth and pigtails falling over her shoulders smiled down at her. Her unbelievably sparkling white dress glistened, highlighting the cooper tones in her skin. It spoke of the time when things were good and pure and innocent.

"Those was happy times," Esther said to herself. "Then Preacha..."

"How my little songbird," he said, patting her on the head. "Come on over here an sit on my lap. Lord, ain't nothin' better than havin' my baby girl right here on my lap."

She slid onto his lap shyly searching his face as his hand smoothed her soft black hair. His large dark hands moved downward and caressed her shoulders and back. That was the moment she wanted to leave. But by then, it was too late.

"You know, Esther," he said. "You jus' like my own daughter. Yessir! I'm mighty proud to have you in my family. You know I love you jus' like my own, don't you?"

"I guess," she said, uncomfortable with the closeness.

"Well, I want to teach you what father's

supposed to do for their lil' girls. Would you like that, Esther?"

She shrugged her shoulders, wishing he'd let her go. Wishing she could disappear. She wanted to run. She wanted to hide, though she didn't really know why.

"What fathers do with their lil' girls is their own secret. Can't nobody know about it. You not even supposed to tell yo' Mama. You understand?"

A head nod up and down, signaled yes. But the word "no" was on the tip of her tongue. She shifted positions on his lap, uncomfortable by the hardness growing between his legs, and his heavy breathing near her ear.

"Come with me," Preacha said, leading her by the hand towards the bed. "Remember this is our little secret," he said, patting her on the hand.

Everything was a slow blur. Esther blinked her eyes hoping the nightmare would end. But when she opened her eyes, Preacha was still there. He was breathing and moaning and moving all over her body.

The urge to scream surged through her body and stalled in her dry throat. The sound refused to release itself into the air. A silent tear rolled down her face as she turned her head, trying to escape the only way she could.

"Shh!" she heard him say, as he covered her mouth with his hand. "Jus' be still, an you gone like it."

She squirmed and wiggled under his weight as the hand tightened over her mouth and he entered her. A pain unlike any she had ever felt before, shot through the center of her body and traveled outward in every direction.

Her body was experiencing the ultimate invasion, as she lay helpless. This profound loss of control over her own body was like dying. It was like Preacha was stabbing her, like he was killing a small but vital part of her…

"What in the world you thinkin' about girl?" Mae Mae said, as she handed Esther a cup of coffee. "You been lookin' at that ole picture since you came in here."

"I was thinkin' how I didn't really know that little girl in the picture," Esther said, moving to sit down on the couch. "It's almost like that little girl is really somebody else."

"Why you say that, Chile?"

"You know why, Mama. You know what Preacha did to me. After all o' these years, I ain't never got over that. That little girl in the picture with that nice little ironed white dress, she was pure and innocent. Preacha took all o' that away from me."

They sat in the shallow light of the room with Esther's words hanging, weighing them down. "You never really knew what that did to me, Mama. You was mad about what Preacha done. But yo' anger didn't have everything to do with me.

"You always carried some deep pain inside that made it hard for you to feel for other folk's. You loved me. God knows how much you loved me. And you really tried to be there for me. But you was never no more there for me than you was for Elijah. But I don't want to talk about Elijah right now. This is about you an me."

Esther's words shocked Mae Mae. A stabbing pain hit her right in the center of her chest. The guilt and suffering from years of abuse, both against her and by her stared her in the face.

For the first time, she could see the pain Esther had suffered. It showed in her eyes. She saw the hurt that had festered for years like a slow cancer. And she realized how much it resembled her own.

As their eyes met, tears erupted from them both. It was as if they were commanded by a powerful force neither of them could control. It drew them together without the necessity for words, as they locked together in a fierce embrace.

Each tear that fell represented years of pain. It was the pain they had both kept to themselves that was pouring forth. It was a pain that had grown quietly and secretly inside of each of them.

Mae Mae took Esther's face in her hands and gently wiped the warm tears from her eyes. She saw in Esther's eyes that the both of them had carried the sins of the past.

"I'm sorry baby," Mae Mae said. "I loved you better than anything in this world. I'm sorry Preacha an Elijah did those things to you. It hurt me jus' like it hurt you.

"I been tryin' all my life to keep on goin' even when somebody hurt me. I always try to put the bad things behin' me. I don't never forget it. But I use it to

Black-Eyed Peas and Cornbread

make me stronger."

Esther shook her head from side to side. "What you think I been doin' Mama. I moved on. I made a life for myself. But I had to carry this hell with me everywhere I went.

"You wasn't able to help me. You was actin' like my pain an yours didn't never happen. You never really just put yo' arms around me after we left Preacha. You said you could've killed him. But you never really dealt with me an my broken heart.

"By the time Elijah forced me to leave Eastend, I felt like I couldn't trust you to believe in me. That's why I left town, Mama. It was as much about you as it was about Preacha an Elijah."

On those words they sat silently in the fading darkness. They held each other as they waited for the newness of the light of morning. It was as if a new day would provide the understanding and forgiveness they so desperately needed.

Chapter 18

The sun peeped shyly from behind the ridges of Beaucatcher Mountain as Mae Mae led Esther by the hand to the outside of the house. Asheville's morning chill lightly caressed their arms. But both of them ignored the cold. They were taken in by the familiar sounds of the Eastend streets.

"Where we goin' Mama? Esther asked. "What you so anxious to show me?"

"You'll see," Mae Mae said, still walking, still leading Esther by the hand.

When Mae Mae finally stopped, she stood for a moment and stared in the direction of a large vacant lot. "Remember this place, Esther?" Mae Mae finally asked.

"I don't know for sure," Esther said, somewhat puzzled. "Ain't this were Ma Letty's house was? Why you bring me here?"

"I don't never want you to forget Ma Letty, Esther. She was like a mother to me. I come here all the time. When I'm worried an hurtin' an sad, this is where I come. There's peace here even with the house gone. I ain't never really been able to find it no where else.

"This family need some peace, Chile. All o' us been through too much."

"Even Elijah?" Esther asked, not knowing what Mae Mae would say.

Mae Mae took a deep breath. She looked around at the green grass that had grown in the place of the house she used to know so well. She moved with Esther towards a patch of grass on a high mound, and they sat down.

"Esther, don't talk to me about Elijah," Mae Mae said. "I can't get over what he done to the people in the world I love the most. If I were to see him right now, I don't know what I'd do."

"What you mean Mama?"

"Never mind. That's something I have to keep to myself," Mae Mae said staring in the opposite direction.

"Well, I been doin' a lot o' thinkin' since Elijah came to New York a year or two ago. That's what finally brought me home."

"Yeah! I been thinkin' a lot myself," said Mae Mae. "You know, Esther," she said thoughtfully. "I keep on rackin' my brain tryin' to figure out what happened to Elijah. God! Maybe I should've loved him just' a little more.

"All the hate seem like it built up in Elijah from the time he was a little baby, Esther. I hated Red so much. I hated bein' pregnant with Elijah. I hated bein' alive. With all that hatin', I jus' didn't have no room for lovin' Elijah.

"God, Esther! I found out that Elijah set the fire that killed Ma Letty. Did you know that? Right here in this very spot, he killed Ma Letty."

"No Mama!!"

"Yeah," Mae Mae said, with tears in her eyes. "An when he told me what he done to you. That's when I told him what I'd do if I ever saw him again."

A. Jean Jackson

There was a silence inside of the grassy space where they sat. They were held inside just like the walls were still there. Both of them could feel it as they breathed in the mountain air and looked out over the whole of Eastend.

"Mama it's true though," Esther said, breaking the silence. "Elijah did some terrible things. But now's the time he really needin' some forgiveness. He told me when he came to New York he was dyin'. We his only family, Mama. He needs us."

Mae Mae looked away staring into the distance. She couldn't really hear or feel what Esther was saying. The thoughts going through her mind could never be revealed to another human soul.

"We got to find him, Esther," Mae Mae said with urgency in her voice. "We got to find Elijah."

They circled and entered at the back side of the building. The smell of sickness directed them inside. For a brief moment, the smell reminded Mae Mae of Red. She turned away, fighting off the urge to throw up.

"Mama, you alright?" Esther asked.

"Yeah. Yeah, I'm a'right. This sick urine smell jus' remind me o' somethin' awful, that's all.

Slowly, hand in hand they walked through the shiny long halls that appeared to lead to nowhere. They dodged all of the sickness, loneliness, hurt and pain that stared at them from the rooms they passed. They trudged along searching the faces for a glimpse of him.

"Where can we find a man named Elijah Redman?" Esther asked, when they reached the end of the hall.

"Right down here," the tall dark woman in white said, leading the way. "Who are ya'll? Elijah's always sayin' he ain't got no family."

"Well, I'm his mama," Mae Mae said. "An this here's his sister."

"Tell you the truth," the woman said, opening his door, showing them in. "I'm glad you showed up when you did. He been in here jus' wastin' away."

With a glance of disbelief, he blinked his eyes to see if the sight before him was real. It was a sight he thought he would never see again.

"Mama, is that you?" Elijah asked, sitting up in his bed. "An Esther you came back. Your really came back."

Esther smiled, though cautiously. Mae Mae stood back looking, still hating, still planning her revenge. Deep down inside, his sickly pale look, made her really want to feel sorry for him. She really wanted to show him the love he needed. But his face, and those dreadful eyes, revealed to her a powerful combination of all of Red's deeds and his.

"Esther, let me speak to Elijah alone for a moment," Mae Mae said, with no feeling in her voice.

"What's wrong, Mama?" Esther said, looking confused.

"Jus' leave us be, Esther!, she shouted "I got business to settle with Elijah."

A. Jean Jackson

He rested way back deep inside the pillows that surrounded his small, frail body. The eyes that had once been bright were now dull, weak and tired. Mae Mae felt pitty as she looked down on him in his bed.   "I told you what I'd do if I saw you again," she said, close to his ear. "Don't think I changed my mind jus' 'casue I'm here with Esther. Seeing ya'll together and rememberin' what you did, make me want to get you even more."

She reached for a pillow resting at the bottom of the bed. In slow motion, almost as if time had stopped just for that moment and in that room, she took the pillow towards his face. And when she looked into his eyes, she found in her reflection. She saw that every ounce of hate she had for Elijah was matched by the pitty he had for her. She saw in the eyes that she had hated since before he was born, only love, peace and forgivenss. And all she could do was cry. She cried loudly, as if a lifetime of hate needed to empty from her soul.

"I know how you feel," Elijah said, calmly. "But Mama, just remember, I'm dying anyway. You'd be doing me a favor and you'd be just speeding up the process. I know I've sinned. I know I've done wrong. And I've asked my God for forgiveness a million times. I've come to know my God in these days of sitting here looking at these walls. And I've learned that with God as my Father, I need to fear nothing.

"What about you Mama? You got anything you sorry for? Have you been forgiven for yo' sins, Mama?"

Black-Eyed Peas and Cornbread

She stood back in silence, surprised by his words. Her thoughts switched immediately from his deeds to her own.

"Yes," she said after a long pause. "I've got things I'm real sorry about. Everybody do, I guess."

"Well just remember Mama, most of us don't know when the end is coming. We all need to seek forgiveness and clean up our lives, just to be ready."

The person speaking to her from the bed was not a person she had ever known before. It was her son, Elijah, but he had a new spirit. It was a man with the life slowly seeping from his body, but he was more alive than she had ever seen him.

"You're right son," she said. "I need to seek my own forgiveness from God and from my children."

She peeped outside the door and called Esther back inside. Her voice had an urgency that not even she understood. Esther reentered more confused than when she left.

"Come here Chile," Mae Mae said softly, taking Esther by the hand and walking towards the bed. She was still crying, but her voice was strong and she was in control.

"Elijah, I ain't never loved you like I should. I ain't never gave you a chance in life. I know all the things you done. You're right. I have to seek forgiveness for my own sins. Years ago, I did somethin' jus' as sinful as anything you ever did, Elijah. Ya'll never knew this. Elijah, I never told you the real truth about why we had to run away from yo' Daddy.

A. Jean Jackson

"I don't remember a day Red wasn't beatin' me. I jus' couldn't take it no more. Wasn't no way to git away unless I killed him. An until now, until I was able to tell you an Esther, I ain't never really forgave myself."

"Why Mama? Why did you have to kill him?" he asked really understanding, but still needing to ask.

"Son I tried to get away once. I ran from him after he killed Jacob. An Red forced me to go back soon after Esther was born. Killin' him was my only way out."

"I got pregnant with you after Red forced me to go back. I hated him so much. It was real hard to love his chile. I'm sorry Elijah. I hope you can understand why that always came between us. Most of all, I hope you can find it in yo' heart to forgive me."

"Yeah Elijah," Esther said, breaking in. "I did a lot o' thinkin' after you came to New York to see me. That's what brought me home. I want this family to love each other. My baby's gone need a real family when it comes."

"I feel the same way," Elijah said, behind his tears. "I need my family now too. I don't want you to leave me here in this place to die by myself. I want to go home. I want to be with my family."

Chapter 19

The sound of pine crackling in the fireplace made the room seem much warmer than it really was. The whiteness that covered the ground as far as the eye could see added to the mood of the holiday season.

They sat together in the dim light of the living room, feeling blessed to be together, yet enjoying the understood silence between them. The simple yet complex beauty of a snowflake peeking inside at Elijah, occupied him totally. This was for him and him alone. It was not to be shared. Not even with his mother.

Mae Mae's thoughts were on her resolutions. And her silent prayer as she sat looking out at the snow, was that Elijah was planning his resolutions too. She hoped that he at least would want to plan for another year.

She pulled up on the arm of her chair and headed for the kitchen. "What time's Esther an Mitch comin' tomorrow with the baby?" she yelled back to Elijah over her shoulder.

"In time for dinner," he said, mustering up a weak smile.

"Well I'm gone put these blackeyed peas on to soak over night. Then, I'm goin' to bed. I got a lot o' cookin' to do tomorrow. I'm gone cook a good ole New Years Day feast for this family."

"OK Mama," he said in a low voice. "Mama," he said, as if he was pulling something from deep inside.

A. Jean Jackson

"Can I talk to you about somethin'?"

"Yeah, Honey. What's wrong, you in too much pain? You been mighty quiet the last few days."

"Yeah, Mama," he said. I'm hurtin' really bad. An I need to ask you a big favor. It's probably more than anyone ever asked you in yo' whole life. But these last few months have been beautiful. I realize now, that I have the kind of family that I can ask anything of."

"What son? You know I'll do anything for you. Just ask."

"Mama, I want you to help me die. I'm sick, I'm tired, and I'm hurtin' more and more everyday. I just want to give up. I don't want to live like this."

"Oh no! Elijah! I thought you were happy. I thought everything was alright. Honey don't ask me to do that. We all just got you back. We all jus' started feelin' what it's really like to be a family."

"I know, Mama. And that's why it's so easy for me to give up now. I know I can give up and rest in peace now 'cause I've been surrounded by love and family. Please, Mama! I beg you. I ain't hardly asked you for nothin' in this life. Please do this one last thing for me."

Tears poured silently down Mae Mae's cheeks. She looked at Elijah and she could see the face he had as a young child. She could see the face, the movement, the smiles that she had missed. She was sorry for the love she had denied him, denied herself for so many years.

"Jus' think about, Mama. Remember, whenever

the time comes, I'm ready to meet my maker. I'm not scared, Mama."

"Let's jus' both go to bed now, son. You'll have a better day tomorrow when Esther and Mitch get here."

"I'm stayin' up for a while," he said. "I want to be sittin' up at midnight when the New Year comes in.

"Happy New Year, Elijah," she said, kissing him on the cheek. "I'll see you in the morning."

As usual, the morning came much too soon. But Mae Mae rose early to prepare for the big family dinner. When she climbed out of bed, she got on her knees to pray.

"God! Please lead me and guide me with what's in my heart. I feel so old, so helpless. I'm responsible for making my children's lives so miserable. Seem like bad, evil times like that jus' go from one generation to another. The evil went from Cora Lee to me and from me to my children. Well, it's got to end some where. I've got to do everything I can to make things better."

She stood slowly, holding on tight, weighted down by the past. Her heart was heavy with the decision being forced upon her. But regardless, today was going to be a good day.

"Lord! That boy still ain't went to bed," she said, as she tipped through the living room. "He must've fell asleep sitting up in the chair last night."

She walked over to the chair and paused for a moment to look at him. As he slept she tried to find the face of the child she had given birth to so long ago. But it wasn't there. It was hidden deep inside of the pale, wrinkled sickness that was taking more of him each day.

Elijah wasn't moving. His limbs and his head hung lifeless from the chair. Mae Mae's heart beat faster as she touched him lightly.

"Son! Elijah, Son you alright!" she said. She shook him. Suddenly, his eyes opened.

"Mama, what's wrong," he said, sitting upright in the chair. "I'm sorry I must've fell asleep here last night. I'm alright Mama, don't worry."

"Lord Chile you scared me, that's all," she said, stroking his weak weightless hand. "Don't be scarin' me like that."

Elijah looked at her like he had never looked at her before. As she rubbed the warmth back into his hand with her own, and the worry slowly disappeared from her face, he knew then, how much he loved her.

"I ain't got time to be botherin' with you boy," she said, kissing him on the cheek as she departed. "I'm gone put on my coffee an sweep my porch like I always do. I got me a lot to do today."

By noon, the steam from her cooking rose from the kitchen and danced about the house. It seemed to defy the coldness outdoors. Pots and pans full of blackeyed peas, ham and yams and collards greens vibrated on the stove to her own special rhythm.

Later in the afternoon, the happy sounds of Esther Mitch and the baby coming through the front door warmed the whole house. It was like an extra piece of wood was put on the fire.

"Esther!" Mae Mae shouted. "That baby so precious! So this here is my grandchild?" she said, taking the baby out of Esther's arms. "Look Elijah! Look here at Little Jacob."

Elijah's face lit up with a smile as bright as the snow outside, when Mae Mae placed the baby in his lap. The smell of the baby's soft skin filled his nostrils. The baby's youth, his innocence brought a smile to Elijah's face.

"Happy New Year!" Elijah whispered in the baby's ear. "Remember, you're the future o' this family Little Jacob."

"Well I hope my family is hungry," Mae Mae shouted, placing platters of food on the table. "'Cause I been slavin' over this stove all day."

"Now you always know I'm gone eat yo' food, Mizz Mae," said Mitch, pulling out a chair at the table for Esther. "That's why I got into this family. "Because of yo' cookin'," he said as they all laughed.

Mae Mae helped Elijah to his seat at the head of the table. The family joined hands and bowed their heads. They awaited the prayer that Mae Mae had longed to pray for a very long time. All of their eyes were closed. But they could see her clearly. They could feel her words.

"God! I am yo' servant," she said loudly. "There are things we do for hate and there are things we are forced to do for love. Thank you for helping my family to finally know the difference. We done had some hard times, Lord. But we ain't lookin' back no more.

A. Jean Jackson

We lookin' ahead. Bless this food on this special day. Amen!"

"Amen!" Elijah shouted, with tears in his eyes.

Later that evening, they said their goodbyes to Esther, Mitch, and Little Jacob. A chill ascended Mae Mae's body as she closed the door behind them. "That was a wonderful day," she said. "It was the best day of my whole life."

"Mine too," Elijah said, smiling.

"Son, how about some leftovers before bedtime. Let me get you some more of those blackeyed peas."

Mae Mae brought a full bowl from the kitchen. The steam warmed her face as she handed it to Elijah. The room was quiet and nothing could be heard but but the spoon hitting the side of the bowl and his chewing. Elijah dozed off to sleep and Mae Mae took the bowl from his hands.

This night, she didn't go to her bed. This night, she waited for complete and total peace to capture the face of her son. And then she took Elijah in her arms and rocked him until daylight crept into the windows.

Made in the USA
Columbia, SC
06 September 2017